# THE LIFE
# AND LOVES
# OF A
# SHE-DEVIL

# THE LIFE AND LOVES OF A 'SHE-DEVIL'

# FAY WELDON

**PANTHEON BOOKS, NEW YORK**

Copyright © 1983 by Fay Weldon

All rights reserved under International and Pan-American Copyright Conventions. Published in the United States by Pantheon Books, a division of Random House, Inc., New York. Originally published in Great Britain by Hodder and Stoughton Limited in 1983.

Library of Congress Cataloging in Publication Data

Weldon, Fay.
The life and loves of a she-devil.
I. Title.
PR6073.E374L5    1984    823'.914    84-7070
ISBN 0-394-53920-6

BOOK DESIGN BY GINA DAVIS

Manufactured in the United States of America

First American Edition

# THE LIFE
# AND LOVES
# OF A
# SHE·DEVIL

Mary Fisher lives in a High Tower, on the edge of the sea: she writes a great deal about the nature of love. She tells lies.

Mary Fisher is forty-three, and accustomed to love. There has always been a man around to love her, sometimes quite desperately, and she has on occasion returned this love, but never, I think, with desperation. She is a writer of romantic fiction. She tells lies to herself, and to the world.

Mary Fisher has $ (US) 754,300 on deposit in a bank in Cyprus, where the tax laws are lax. This is the equivalent of £502,867 sterling, 1,931,009 German marks, 1,599,117 Swiss francs, 185,055,050 yen, and so forth, it hardly matters which. A woman's life is what it is, in any corner of the world. And wherever you go it is the same—to them that hath, such as Mary Fisher, shall be given, and to them that hath not, such as myself, even that which they have shall be taken away.

Mary Fisher earned all her money herself. Her first husband, Jonah, told her that capitalism was immoral, and she believed him, having a gentle and pliable nature. Otherwise no doubt by now Mary Fisher would have a substantial portfolio of investments. As it is, she owns four houses and these are cumulatively worth—depending on the state of the property market—anything between half a million and a million dollars. A house, of course, only means anything in financial terms if there is anyone to buy it, or if you can bear to sell it. Otherwise a house can only be somewhere to live, or somewhere where those connected with you can live. With luck, the ownership of property brings peace of mind; without this luck it brings aggravation and discontent. I wish unluck in property matters on Mary Fisher.

Mary Fisher is small and pretty and delicately formed, prone to fainting and weeping and sleeping with men while pretending that she doesn't.

Mary Fisher is loved by my husband, who is her accountant.

I love my husband and I hate Mary Fisher.

**2** Now. Outside the world turns: tides surge up the cliffs at the foot of Mary Fisher's tower, and fall again. In Australia the great gum trees weep their bark away; in Calcutta myriad flickers of human energy ignite and flare and die; in California the surfers weld their souls with foam and flutter off into eternity. And I am fixed here and now, trapped in my body, pinned to one particular spot, hating Mary Fisher. It is all I can do. Hate obsesses and transforms me: it is my singular attribution. I have only recently discovered it.

Better to hate than to grieve. I sing in praise of hate, and all its attendant energy. I sing a hymn to the death of love.

If you travel inland from Mary Fisher's tower, down its sweep of graveled drive (the gardener is paid $110 a week, which is low in any currency), through the windswept avenue of sadly blighted poplars (perhaps this is his revenge), then off her property and on to the main road and through the rolling western hills, and down to the great wheat plain, and on and on for sixty miles or so, you come to the suburbs and the house where I live: to the little green garden where my and Bobbo's children play. There are a thousand more or less similar houses, to the east, north, west, and south: we are in the middle, exactly in the middle, of a place called Eden Grove. A suburb. Neither town nor country: intermediate. Green, leafy, prosperous, and, some say, beautiful. I grant you it is a better place to live than a street in downtown Bombay.

I know how central I am in this centerless place because I spend a lot of time with maps. I need to know the geographical detail of misfortune. The distance between my house and Mary Fisher's tower is one hundred and eight kilometers, or sixty-seven miles.

The distance between my house and the station is three-quarters of a mile, and from my house to the shops is seven hundred and twenty-five yards. Unlike the majority of my neighbors I do not drive a car. I am less well coordinated than they. I have failed four driving tests. I might as well walk, I say, since there is so little else to do, once you have swept the corners and polished the surfaces, in this place which was planned as paradise. How wonderful, I say, and they believe me, to stroll through heaven.

Bobbo and I live at No. 19 Nightbird Drive. It is a select street in the best part of Eden Grove. The house is very new: we are its first occupants. It is clean of resonance. Bobbo and I have two bathrooms, and picture windows, and we wait for the trees to grow: presently, you see, we will even have privacy.

Eden Grove is a friendly place. My neighbors and I give dinner parties for one another. We discuss things, rather than ideas; we exchange information, not theories; we keep ourselves steady by thinking about the particular. The general is frightening. Go too far into the past and there is nonexistence, too far into the future and there you find the same. The present must be exactly balanced. These days spare ribs are served, Chinese style, daringly, with paper napkins and finger bowls. It smacks of change. The men nod and laugh: the women tremble and smile and drop dishes.

It is a good life. Bobbo tells me so. He comes home less often, so does not say so as often as he did.

Does Mary Fisher love my husband? Does she return his love? Does she look into his eyes, and speak to him without words?

I was taken to visit her once, and stumbled over the carpet—a true Kashmiri rug valued at $2,540—as I approached her. I am six feet two inches tall, which is fine for a man but not for a woman. I am as dark as Mary Fisher is fair, and have one of those jutting jaws that tall, dark women often have, and eyes sunk rather far back into my face, and a hooked nose. My shoulders are broad and bony and my hips broad and fleshy, and the muscles in my legs are well developed. My arms, I swear, are too short for my body. My nature and my looks do not agree. I was unlucky, you might think, in the great lottery that is woman's life.

When I tripped over the rug Mary Fisher smirked, and I saw her eyes dart to Bobbo's, as if this were a scene they had already envisaged.

"Tell me about your wife," she would have murmured, after love.

"Clumsy," he would have said. He might have added, if I was lucky, "No beauty, but a good soul." Yes, I think he would have said that, if only to excuse himself and deny me. A man cannot be expected to be faithful to a wonderful mother and a good wife—such concepts lack the compulsion of the erotic.

Would he also have remarked, in guilty and excited mirth, "She has four moles on her chin and from three of them hairs grow"? I imagine so; who could resist it, giggling and squealing and tickling in bed, after love, assessing life?

I am quite sure at some time or other Bobbo would have said, in the manner of husbands, "I love her. I love her but I'm not *in* love with her: not the way I'm in love with you. Do you understand?" And Mary Fisher would have nodded, understanding very well.

I know what life is like: I know what people are like. I know that we all make common cause in self-deception and wishful thinking, and who more so than adulterous lovers? I have time to think about it, when the dishes are done, and the house is quiet, and life ticks by, and there is nothing to do except wonder whether Bobbo and Mary Fisher are together *now, now*—how strange time seems! And I think and think and I act each role, sometimes him, sometimes her. It makes me feel part of the whole both make. I, who have been made nothing. And then Bobbo rings and says he won't be home, and the children come back from school, and a strange familiar silence descends upon the house, a thick, white muffling blanket thrown over our lives: and even when the cat catches a mouse, the yowls and yelps seem to come from a distant place, another world.

Bobbo is a good-looking man, and I am lucky to have him. The neighbors often remark upon it. "You are so lucky, having someone like Bobbo." Not surprising, their eyes go on to say, that he's away every now and then. Bobbo is five feet ten, four inches shorter than I am. He is six inches taller than Mary Fisher, who has size 4 feet and last year spent $1,200.50 on shoes. In bed with me, all the same, Bobbo has no potency problems. He shuts his eyes. For all I know he shuts his eyes when he's in bed with her, but I don't really think so. It's not how I envisage it.

What I think is that the other women up and down Eden Grove are better than I am at telling themselves lies. Their own husbands are away often enough. How otherwise but by lies do they live, do they keep their self-esteem? Sometimes, of course, not even lies can protect them. They are found hanging in the garage, or cold and overdosed in the marital bed. Love has killed them, murderous in its own death throes, flailing and biting and poisonous.

And how, especially, do ugly women survive, those whom the world pities? The dogs, as they call us. I'll tell you; they live as I do, outfacing truth, hardening the skin against perpetual humiliation, until it's as tough and cold as a crocodile's. And we wait for old age to equalize all things. We make good old women.

My mother was pretty enough, and ashamed of me. I could see it in her eyes. I was her eldest child. "The image of your father," she'd say. She'd married again, of course, by then. She'd left my father long ago, far behind, despised. My two half-sisters both took after her; they were delicate, fine-boned things. I liked them. They knew how to charm, and they charmed even me. "Little ugly duckling," my mother said to me once, almost weeping, smoothing my wiry hair. "What are we to do with you? What's to become of you?" I think perhaps she would have loved me, if she could. But ugly and discordant things revolted her: she couldn't help it. She said as much often enough: not of me, particularly, of course, but I knew the patterns of her thought, I knew what she meant. I was born, I sometimes think, with nerve endings not inside but outside my skin: they shivered and twanged. I grew lumpish and brutish in the attempt to seal them over, not to know too much.

And I could never, you see, even for my mother's sake, learn just to smile and stay quiet. My mind struck keys like a piano dreadfully out of tune, randomly played, never quiet. She christened me Ruth, wanting, I think, even in my first days, to forget me if she could. A short, dismissive, sorrowful name. My little half-sisters were called Jocelyn and Miranda. They married well, and disappeared, no doubt into contentment, bathed in the glow of the world's admiration.

**3** Mary Fisher, dweller in the High Tower! What's for dinner tonight? Perhaps you don't even know. Perhaps you leave that to the servants. And who's for company? Perhaps you have yet more lovers to choose from: to gaze out with you, through plate-glass windows, over harbor and sea; to watch the moon rise and the sky turn color? Perhaps you never eat, but with a mind half on food, and half on love to come? Lucky you! But tonight, whoever else, you shan't have Bobbo. Tonight Bobbo is eating with me.

I shall open the French windows from the dining room onto the garden; that is, if the wind doesn't get up. We have some very pretty night-scented stock growing up the side of the garage. We have double-glazing.

The bill for keeping Mary Fisher's windows clean was $295.75, only last month. The sum was transferred from the bank in Cyprus into Mary Fisher's housekeeping account. Bobbo, on the occasions he is home, often brings Mary Fisher's accounts with him. I don't sleep much on the nights he is with me: I get out of bed, quietly, and go into his study and look through Mary Fisher's life. Bobbo sleeps soundly. He comes home to rest, really. To catch up on lost sleep.

I clean our windows myself: sometimes to be tall is quite an advantage.

Tonight, at No. 19 Nightbird Drive, we're going to have mushroom soup, chicken vol-au-vents, and chocolate mousse.

Bobbo's parents are coming to visit. He does not want to upset them, so he will play the quiet suburban husband and sit, for once, at the head of the table. He will look out onto wallflowers and hollyhocks and vines. I like gardening. I like to control nature, and make things beautiful.

Bobbo is doing very well in the world. He has become successful. Once he worked humbly as an official in the Revenue Department but then he resigned, threw caution to the winds, risked his pension, and began to do private tax work. Now he earns a great deal of money. It suits him to keep me tucked away in Eden Grove. Bobbo has a pleasant apartment in the center of the city, ten miles farther still to the east, ten miles farther from Mary Fisher, where he gives occasional parties for his clients, where he first met Mary Fisher face-to-face, where he stays overnight when business presses. So he says. I very seldom go to Bobbo's apartment, or his office. I let it be known I am too busy. It would be embarrassing to Bobbo if his smart new clients saw me. We both know it. Bobbo's graceless wife! All very well, I daresay, for an income-tax collector; hardly for a tax expert working in the private field, growing rich.

Mary Fisher, I hope that tonight you are eating canned red salmon and the can has spoiled and you get botulin poisoning. But such hope is in vain. Mary Fisher eats fresh salmon, and in any case her delicate palate could be trusted to detect poison, no matter how undetectable it might be in other, cruder mouths. How delicately, how swiftly she would spit the erring mouthful out and save herself!

Mary Fisher, I hope such a wind arises tonight that the plate-glass windows of the tower crack and the storm surges in, and you die drowning and weeping and in terror.

9

I make puff pastry for the chicken vol-au-vents, and when I have finished circling out the dough with the brim of a wineglass, making wafer rounds, I take the thin curved strips the cutter left behind and mold them into a shape much like the shape of Mary Fisher, and turn the oven high, high, and crisp the figure in it until such a stench fills the kitchen that even the fan cannot remove it. Good.

I hope the tower burns and Mary Fisher with it, sending the smell of burning flesh out over the waves. I would go and fire the place myself, but I don't drive. I can only get to the tower if Bobbo drives me there and he no longer does so. Sixty-five miles. He says it is much too far.

Bobbo, parting Mary Fisher's smooth little legs, shiny calved, shiny thighed, inserting his finger, as his habit is, where presently his concentrated self will follow.

I know he does the same to her as he does to me, because he told me so. Bobbo believes in honesty. Bobbo believes in love.

"Be patient," he says, "I don't intend to leave you. It's just that I'm in love with her and at the moment must act accordingly." Love, he says! Love! Bobbo talks a lot about love. Mary Fisher writes about nothing but love. All you need is love. I assume I love Bobbo because I am married to him. Good women love their husbands. But love, compared to hate, is a pallid emotion. Fidgety and troublesome, and making for misery.

My children come in from the midsummer garden. A pigeon pair. The boy, slight like my mother, and like her given to complaints. The girl, big and lumpy, as I am, voicing a vindictiveness that masks the despair of too much feeling. The dog and the cat follow after. The guinea pig rustles and snuffles in its corner. I have just turned out its cage. The chocolate for the mousse bubbles and melts in the pan. This is the happiness, the completeness of domestic, suburban life. It is what we should be happy with: our destiny. Out of the gutter of wild desire onto the smooth lawns of married love.

Sez you, as I heard my mother's mother say, on her deathbed, when promised eternal life by the attendant priest.

**4** Bobbo's mother Brenda stole around the outside of her son's house at No. 19 Nightbird Drive. She had a playful disposition, which her son had not inherited. Brenda meant to surprise Ruth by pressing her nose against a window-pane. "Coo-ee, I'm here," she would mouth through the glass. "The monster, the mother-in-law!" Thus she would apologize for her difficult role in the family and get the evening off, so she imagined, to a good start, any tension there might be dissolving into laughter.

Brenda's little heels sank into the smooth lawn, spoiling both them and it. The grass was newly mown. Ruth liked mowing the lawn. She could push the mower with one powerful hand, and the job was swiftly and easily done, while her littler neighbors perspired and complained, coping, as they always had to, with grass left to grow too long in the belief, dashed weekly and reborn weekly, that mowing the grass was what husbands did.

Bobbo's mother peered into the kitchen window where the mushroom soup simmered, waiting for its dash of cream and splash of sherry, and nodded her approval. She liked things to be properly done—so long as someone else did it. She looked through the open French windows into the dining room, where the table was laid for four and the candles were in their sticks, the silver dishes polished and the sideboard dusted, and sighed her admiration. Ruth was good at polishing. One rub of the powerful fingers and stains disappeared. Brenda was obliged to use an electric toothbrush to keep her own silver nice—a lengthy and irritating business—and she envied Ruth perhaps this one thing: her way with silver.

Bobbo's mother Brenda did not envy Ruth's being married to Bobbo. Brenda did not love Bobbo and never had. She quite liked Bobbo, and quite liked her husband; but even there, feelings were elusive.

The smell of night-scented stock filled the air.

"How nicely she does everything," said Bobbo's mother to her husband, Angus. "How lucky Bobbo is!" Angus stood on the path, waiting for his wife's playfulness to abate, and for her to stop looking in windows. Brenda wore beige silk and gold bracelets and liked to feel timeless. Angus wore a brownish check suit and a yellow-ocher shirt and a blue spotted tie. No matter how rich or poor they happened to be, Brenda always looked a little too elegant, and Angus just a little absurd. Brenda had a little tip-tilted nose and too-wide eyes, and Angus a great fleshy nose and narrow eyes.

Bobbo wore gray suits and white shirts and pale ties and was careful always to look serious and neutral, biding his time, concealing his power. His nose was straight and strong and his eyes just right.

Brenda looked into the family room and saw the two children watching television. The remains of an early supper stood on the table. They were washed, combed, and ready for bed: they seemed happy, although graceless. But then with Ruth for a mother what could you expect?

"She's such a good mother," whispered Brenda to Angus, beckoning him closer to admire. "You have to respect her."

Brenda shook her heels free of clinging earth and went around to the laundry room where Bobbo was at that moment removing an ironed, folded shirt from a neat pile. He wore only his underwear, but hadn't Brenda bathed him when he'd been a little boy? Can a mother be frightened of her son's nakedness?

Brenda did not notice the neat little bite marks on her son's upper arm: or perhaps she did, and assumed they were insect bites. They certainly could not have been made by Ruth's teeth, which were broad, heavy, and irregular.

"She's such a good wife," said Bobbo's mother, moved almost to tears. "Look at that ironing!" Bobbo's mother never ironed if she could help it. In the good times indeed, she and Angus liked to live in hotels, simply because there'd be a valet service. "And what a good husband Bobbo has turned out to be!" If she thought her son was narcissistic, staring so long in the mirror, she kept her thoughts to herself.

But Bobbo looked in the mirror at his clear, elegant eyes, his intelligent brow, and his slightly bruised mouth, and hardly saw himself at all: he saw the man whom Mary Fisher loved.

Bobbo, as he dressed, was working out in his head a monetary scale for lovemaking. He felt happier when he could put a fiscal value to things. He was not stingy: he was happy enough to spend money. He merely felt that life and money were the same thing. His father had implied it often enough.

"Time is money," Angus would say, hurrying his son off to school, out of the house. "Life is time, and time is money." Sometimes Bobbo would have to walk, because there was no money for the bus. Sometimes he'd go by chauffeur and Rolls-Royce. Angus had made two millions and lost three during the course of Bobbo's childhood. A life full of ups and downs for a growing boy! "In the time you take to do that," he'd say to the toddler Bobbo, trying to lace his tiny shoes with untrained fingers, "I could make a thousand dollars."

A monetary scale for lovemaking, Bobbo thought, would have to set the sum of earning-capacity-wasted plus energy-consumed against the balance of pleasure-gained plus renewed-creativity. A cabinet minister's coitus, however feeble, could work out at some $200, a housewife's entr'acte, however energetic, a mere $25. An act of love with Mary Fisher, a high earner and energetic with it, would be worth $500. An act of love with his wife would be graded at $75, but of course occurred more often so unfortunately would yield a diminishing return. The more often sex with a particular person happened, Bobbo believed, the less it was worth.

Bobbo's mother extracted her heels once more from the well-tended earth of the new lawn, beckoned her husband, and with him made her way to the front of the house. She looked into the living room and there, behold, was Ruth's mountainous back, bent over the record player, arranging a pleasant selection of predinner and postdinner music.

Ruth straightened up, knocking her head against the oak beam over the fireplace. The house had been designed for altogether smaller occupants.

As Ruth's mother-in-law prepared to flatten her nose against the windowpane and be playful, Ruth turned. Even through the distorting glass it was clear that she had been crying. Her face was puffy and her eyes swollen. "The suburban blues!" murmured Brenda to Angus. "It affects even the happiest!" As they watched, Ruth clawed wild hands to heaven, somewhere above the sea-green ceiling, as if entreating the descent of some dreadful god, some necessary destiny.

"I think she's a little more upset than usual," said Bobbo's mother, unwillingly. "I hope Bobbo is being good to her," and she and Bobbo's father went to sit on the low bench outside the house and stare into the deepening evening that fell over Nightbird Drive, and talk in a desultory way about their own and other people's lives.

"We'll give her time to calm down," said Bobbo's mother. "Dinner parties, even when they're only family, can be quite a strain!"

Bobbo's mother had a calm word and a quiet and pleasant thought for every occasion. No one could understand whence Bobbo's questing, striving, complaining nature came. Bobbo's father shared his wife's capacity for positive thinking: sixty-six and two-thirds of the time such thinking was justified. Things often turn out for the best, if you expect they will: then all you have to do is leave well enough alone. But Bobbo, unlike his parents, did not like leaving things to chance. Bobbo's ambition was a one hundred percent success rate in life.

Bobbo finished dressing. He took his laundered, folded clothes for granted. When he stayed with Mary Fisher, the manservant, Garcia, saw to these things; that Bobbo took for granted, too.

"What is Mary Fisher having for supper?" wondered Bobbo, as his wife had earlier, and longed to be one of the delicate morsels his mistress put into her mouth. Ah, to be absorbed, incorporated! A slice of smoked salmon, a segment of orange, a drop of champagne!

These were the delicacies that Mary Fisher loved to eat, working out the fantasies of others. Fastidious, impossible Mary Fisher! "A little smoked salmon," she'd say, "really costs no more than a large quantity of canned tuna. And it tastes so much nicer."

It was half a lie and half the truth; it was like so much that Mary Fisher said, and wrote.

Bobbo went into the living room and discovered his large wife clawing at empty air.

"Why are you crying?" he asked.

"Because I bumped my head," she said, and he accepted the lie because his parents would be there any minute, and he had, besides, very little interest anymore in what his wife said or did, or why she cried. He forgot Ruth and wondered, as these days he often did, what exactly was the nature of the relationship between Mary Fisher and Garcia, her manservant. Garcia sliced the smoked salmon, uncorked the champagne, and polished the wide glass panes of the lower floors inside and out. Other household tasks, more menial, he delegated to the maids. Garcia was paid $300 per week, which was twice what live-in men-servants were customarily paid by other of Bobbo's clients. Garcia carried little pots of coffee to his mistress and put them on the great glass table on its pale steel pier, upon which Mary Fisher wrote her novels, on thin, thin paper with clear red ink. Her writing was spidery and tiny. Garcia was tall and fleshy and dark and young, and his fingers were long and sometimes Bobbo wondered where they strayed. Garcia was twenty-five and just the look on him sent Bobbo's mind at once to sexual speculation.

"But Bobbo," Mary Fisher would say, "surely you aren't jealous! Garcia's young enough to be my son."

"Oedipus was pretty young, too," was Bobbo's reply, making Mary Fisher laugh. How pretty her laugh was and how easily it came. Bobbo wanted no one to hear it but himself. Yet how could he possibly be with her all the time? Certainly there was no other way of keeping her to himself and ensuring her fidelity but by being there. Yet Bobbo had money to earn, work to do, children to father, and a wife, clumsy and weeping and boring though she might be, to husband. He had undertaken marriage: he would see it through. And since he suffered, so would Ruth.

His wife seemed to him to be immeasurably large, and to have grown larger since he told her of his love for Mary Fisher. He asked her if she was putting on weight, and she said no, and stood on the scales to prove it. Two hundred and two pounds. A pound or so less, even, than usual! It could only be in his mind, then, that she loomed larger.

Bobbo put on a record. He thought it might drown the sound of his wife's crying. He chose Vivaldi to soothe himself and her. The *Four Seasons*. He wished she would not weep. What did she expect of him? He had never claimed to love her. Or had he? He could hardly remember.

Ruth left the room. He heard the click of the oven opening: he heard a little cry, a crash. She had burned her fingers. The vol-au-vents were on the floor—he knew it. And so small a distance to carry them—from the oven to the table!

Bobbo turned up the volume of the music and went in to find chicken and cream sauce and pastry on the linoleum floor and the dog and the cat already scavenging. He kicked the animals into the garden and pushed Ruth into a chair and told her not to upset the children, who were upset enough by her behavior as it was, and scraped everything up methodically and as hygieni-cally as possible, reconstituting if not individual pastry cases then at least a suggestion of a large, single, chicken-filled flan. It was in the interests of hygiene that Bobbo left a thin film of food upon the floor. He estimated its value at some $2.

He required the cat and the dog to come and lick up the film, but both were now sulking outside and would not come back in. Instead they sat upon the wall, next to his parents, and like them waited for the domestic climate to change.

"Do stop crying," pleaded Bobbo in the kitchen. "Why do you make such a fuss about everything? It's only my parents coming to dinner. They don't expect all this effort. They'd be perfectly happy with a simple meal."

"No, they wouldn't. But I'm not crying because of that."

"Then what?"

"You know."

Ah, Mary Fisher. He did indeed know. He tried reason.

"You didn't expect me, when I married you, never to love anyone again?"

"That is exactly what I expected. It is what everyone expects."

She had been cheated, and knew it.

"But you're not like everyone, Ruth."

"You mean I'm a freak."

"No," he said, cautiously and kindly. "I mean we are all individuals."

"But we're married. That makes us one flesh."

"Our marriage was rather one of convenience, my dear. I think we both acknowledged that at the time."

"Convenient for you."

He laughed.

"Why are you laughing?"

"Because you think in clichés and talk in clichés."

"I suppose Mary Fisher doesn't?"

"Of course she doesn't. She is a creative artist."

Andy and Nicola, the children, appeared in the kitchen door: he little and light, she large and looming. The wrong way around. He seemed more girlish than she. Bobbo blamed Ruth for having got the children wrong. He felt their mother had done it on purpose. His heart bled for them. Children open up exquisite nerves and twang them daily, painfully. He wished they had never been born, even while he loved them. They stood between him and Mary Fisher and he had strange dreams in which they came to sorry ends.

"Can I have a doughnut?" asked Nicola. Her response to domestic crisis was to ask for food. She was very overweight. The expected answer, "No," in its uttering, would set up a counterirritant and thus save her parents from more distress. They would be so busy chiding her they would forget to chide each other, or so she believed, wrongly.

"I have a splinter," said Andy. "Look, I'm limping!"

He demonstrated, walking through the film of food, limping on into the living room, treading sauce into the carpet. It was autumn green, toning prettily and safely with avocado walls and sea-green ceiling. Bobbo reckoned the greasy footprints would add $30 to the cleaning bill. Come its annual overhaul, the carpet would now have to go for special and not regular cleaning.

Outside, Angus and Brenda decided that Ruth would by now have recovered her composure. They left their wall and came up the garden path and rang the forest chimes of the front door. *Pling-plong!*

"Please don't embarrass me in front of my parents," begged Bobbo, and Ruth began to weep the harder: she uttered great gulping sobs and heaved her giant shoulders. Even her tears seemed bigger and more watery than other people's. Mary Fisher, thought Bobbo, wept nice neat little tears, which had an altogether stronger surface tension than his wife's and would surely be worth more on the open matrimonial market. If only there were such a thing, he would trade Ruth in at once.

"Come in," he said to his parents at the front door. "Come in! How wonderful to see you both! Ruth has been peeling onions. She's a little tearful, I'm afraid."

Ruth ran up to her room. When Mary Fisher ran, her footsteps were light and bright. Ruth's weight swayed from one massive leg to another and shook the house each time it fell. Houses in Eden Grove were designed not just for little people but for altogether lighter ones.

**5** Now. In Mary Fisher's novels, which sell by the hundred thousand in glittery pink-and-gold covers, little staunch heroines raise tearful eyes to handsome men, and by giving them up, gain them. Little women can look up to men. But women of six feet two have trouble doing so.

And I tell you this: I am jealous! I am jealous of every little, pretty woman who ever lived and looked up since the world began. I am, in fact, quite eaten up by jealousy, and a fine, lively, hungry emotion it is. But *why* should I care, you ask? Can't I just live in myself and forget that part of my life and be content? Don't I have a home, and a husband to pay the bills, and children to look after? Isn't that enough? "No!" is the answer. I want, I crave, I die to be part of that other erotic world, of choice and desire and lust. It isn't love I want; it is nothing so simple. What I want is to take everything and return nothing. What I want is power over the hearts and pockets of men. It is all the power we can have, down here in Eden Grove, in paradise, and even that is denied me.

I stand in my bedroom, our bedroom, Bobbo's and my bedroom, and compose my face the sooner to return to my matrimonial duties, to wifedom and motherhood, and my in-laws.

To this end I recite the Litany of the Good Wife. It goes like this:

I must pretend to be happy when I am not; for everyone's sake.

I must make no adverse comment on the manner of my existence; for everyone's sake.

I must be grateful for the roof over my head and the food on my table, and spend my days showing it, by cleaning and cooking and jumping up and down from my chair; for everyone's sake.

I must make my husband's parents like me, and my parents like him; for everyone's sake.

I must consent to the principle that those who earn most outside the home deserve most inside the home; for everyone's sake.

I must build up my husband's sexual confidence, I must not express any sexual interest in other men, in private or in public; I must ignore his way of diminishing me by publicly praising women younger, prettier, and more successful than I, and sleeping with them in private, if he can; for everyone's sake.

I must render him moral support in all his undertakings, however immoral they may be, for the marriage's sake. I must pretend in all matters to be less than he.

I must love him through wealth and poverty, through good times and bad, and not swerve in my loyalty to him, for everyone's sake.

But the Litany doesn't work. It doesn't soothe: it incenses. I swerve: my loyalty swerves! I look inside myself: I find hate, yes: hate for Mary Fisher, hot, strong, and sweet: but not a scrap of love, not the faintest, wriggling tendril. I have fallen out of love with Bobbo! I ran upstairs, loving, weeping. I will run downstairs, unloving, not weeping.

**6** "But why was she crying?" asked Brenda of Bobbo, as Ruth lumbered upstairs and the house shook. "Is it the time of the month?"

"I expect so," said Bobbo.

"Such a nuisance for a woman," said Brenda, and Angus coughed a little, embarrassed at the turn the conversation was taking.

Presently Ruth came down, smiling, and served the soup.

Twelve years now since Bobbo first met Ruth. She was one of the girls working in Angus's typing pool. Angus was in the stationery business, working up to his second million, which the introduction of value-added tax was later to whittle away to nothing. Angus and Brenda were for once living in a house, not a hotel, which Bobbo appreciated, although he himself was away at business school. Graduate studies go on for many years, keeping the son (it is usually a son) unusually dependent upon the father.

Ruth was a helpful, willing girl, able to concentrate and not forever staring at her reflection in mirrors. If anything, Ruth avoided mirrors. She lived away from home, although still in her teens. Her bedroom had been needed to accommodate her step-father's model train set. She and the train could not safely share a room, because of her clumsiness and the delicacy and sensitivity of the equipment. One of them had to go, and Ruth was the easier to move. It can take months to adjust train tracks properly and permanently: a young woman can settle anywhere.

So Ruth had taken up residence in a hostel mostly inhabited by shop girls, a particularly light and fine breed of young woman. The belts that cinched their tiny waists would scarcely encompass one of Ruth's thighs.

The leaving of the childhood home had been unemotional: it was obvious to everyone, including Ruth, that she had outgrown the place. She did not like to make a fuss. Her school had been a convent, run by nuns of the more superstitious, less intellectual kind; it concentrated on teaching the female and household graces, and examinations, apart from those in shorthand-typing, were not taken. The training encouraged stoicism, not selfish emotions or attention-seeking tears.

Ruth's half-sisters Miranda and Jocelyn did well enough at St. Martha's, especially in Greek dancing, which they demonstrated very sweetly at end-of-term concerts. Ruth was useful, too, on such occasions, shifting props. "You see," the nuns said, "everyone has a value. There is a place for everyone in God's wonderful creation."

Shortly after Ruth moved into the hostel, her mother left home. Perhaps she, too, felt driven into a corner by the ever-growing train set, or was disappointed by the lack of sexual enthusiasm so often displayed by those who get caught up in this rewarding hobby, or perhaps it was—as Ruth imagined—that the sudden absence of the daughter set the mother free. At any rate Ruth's mother ran off with a mining engineer to western Australia, on the other side of the world, taking Miranda and Jocelyn with her, and Ruth's stepfather presently made do with a woman of fewer expectations, who saw no particular reason why Ruth should visit. Ruth, after all, was not a blood relative, not remotely family.

These facts, coming to Brenda's notice by way of Angus, made her feel sorry for the girl.

"She needs a helping hand!" said Brenda.
Ruth was always the one at the switchboard whenever Brenda called up, early, late, or in the lunch hour, courteous, calm, and efficient. The other girls would be out shopping for little scarves and earrings and eye shadow and so forth and all on Angus's time (no wonder he was so often bankrupt); but never Ruth.
"I was once an ugly duckling," Brenda said to Angus, then. "I know what it feels like."
"She's not an ugly duckling," said Angus. "Ugly ducklings turn into swans."
"I think," said Brenda, "the girl needs a proper home at this, the turning point in her life. She could stay with us. I could help her make the most of herself and she could do a little cooking and cleaning in the evenings, after work, in return. And I really have to have someone for the ironing. She would pay rent, too, of course. She is a very proud girl. Probably about a third of her wages."
"There isn't room," said Angus. The house they lived in was very small, which was how they both felt comfortable. But Brenda pointed out that while Bobbo was at college his room was empty during term-time.
"It's wrong," she said. "An empty room just *feels* wrong."
"You've lived in so many hotels," he said, "you're beginning to think like a hotel manager. But I know what you mean."

Brenda and Angus both felt, but did not quite like to say, that Bobbo's childhood and dependency had been going on for a long time: for too long, in fact. His room should by now be free, surely, for them to use as they wished. Parenthood could not go on forever. And if they wished to fill the room up, Ruth would do the filling very well indeed. "Bobbo can always sleep on the sofa," said Brenda. "It's very comfortable."

Bobbo was surprised and annoyed, coming home for Christmas, to be offered a sofa for a bed, and to find his old schoolbooks moved out of his cupboard to make way for Ruth's flat, trodden-down shoes.

"Look upon Ruth as a sister," said Brenda. "The sister you never had!"

But Bobbo had that preoccupation, common to the only child, a fascination with sibling incest, and took his mother's words as justification for the fulfilling of his fantasies and crept into what after all was his own bed, by dead of night. Ruth was warm and soft and broad and the sofa was cold and hard and narrow. He liked her. She never laughed at him or despised his sexual per-formance, as did Audrey Singer, the girl whom Bobbo currently loved. Bobbo felt that his seduction of Ruth, this vast, obliging mountain, served Audrey right.
It was sexual suicide of the most dramatic kind.
"See what you have done!" he said, in his heart, to Audrey.
"See what you have driven me to! Ruth!"
"See," he said to his mother, in his heart, killing off any number of birds with one stone, "see what happens when you turn me out of my own room, my own bed. I'll simply climb back into it, no matter who's there."

Ruth was happy enough with the arrangement. She hugged the knowledge of her secret love to her heart, and felt healed, and a great deal more like everyone else, just taller, which wasn't noticeable when she was lying down. When her stepfather's new wife rang at Christmas to see how she was getting on she was able to reply, with truth, that she was getting on perfectly well, thus enabling the guilty couple to forget her properly. Ruth's mother presently wrote to say this would be the last letter ever, since her new husband wished her to put her past behind her, and they both now belonged to a wonderful new religion which required total obedience from the wife to the husband. In such acquiescence, wrote Ruth's mother, lay peace. She gave her blessing (and the Master's, too, for she had been allowed to consult him personally about Ruth: the Master was the Oneness's representative on this earth as the wife was the husband's representative) and was thankful that Ruth was now fully grown and able to look after herself. She was more worried about Miranda and Jocelyn, who were still so young, but the Master had told her everything would be all right. This letter was a last, final, loving good-bye.

"Our parents," said Bobbo, "are sent to try us!" He enjoyed Ruth's dependence upon him: the way her dark, deep, bright eyes followed him about the room. He loved to sleep with her; she was a warm, dark, eternal sanctuary and if the light was on he could always shut his eyes.
"Perhaps they'll get married," said Brenda to Angus, "and both move out."
Ruth used up rather more hot water than Brenda had anticipated, especially in the bath. In hotels hot water comes free, or appears to.
"I hardly think so," said Angus. "A boy like Bobbo needs to marry wisely, with an eye to money and connections."
"I had neither," said Brenda, "and yet you married me!" And they kissed, longing to be alone together, to be without the younger generation.

Bobbo went back to college, passed the last of his accountancy exams, came home, and contracted hepatitis. Ruth found that she was pregnant.

"They'll have to get married," said Brenda. "I'm far too old to be nursing an invalid." Ruth was sleeping on the sofa while Bobbo was ill, and she had broken its springs.

"Marriage!" said Bobbo, appalled.

"She's a peach among women," said Brenda. "I don't know how your father will manage without her. She's efficient and conscientious and *good.*"
"But what will people *say?*"

Brenda pretended not to hear and put the house up for sale. She and Angus were moving back into a hotel, now Bobbo could stand on his own feet. Audrey Singer announced her engagement to another. Bobbo drank half a bottle of whiskey, had a bad relapse, and married Ruth when she was five months pregnant. Hepatitis is a depressing and debilitating illness, and it seemed to Bobbo, at the time, that his mother was right and one wife was much like another. The great advantage of Ruth was that she was *there.*

Ruth wore a white satin wedding gown to the Register Office and Bobbo realized perhaps he was wrong. There could be a considerable difference between one wife and another. He thought he saw people sniggering. As soon as the baby was born, she conceived the next.

After that Bobbo insisted that Ruth should wear a coil and looked around for more suitable recipients of his affection and sexual energy. As the effects of hepatitis faded, he found them easily enough. He did not like to be dishonest or hypocritical and would always tell Ruth what had happened and what would happen next, if he could manage it. He told her that she, too, was free to experiment sexually.

"We'll have an open marriage," he'd told her before they were married. She was four months into pregnancy and still being rather sick.

"Of course," she said. "What does that mean?"

"That we must both live our lives to the full and always be honest with each other. Marriage must surround our lives, not circumvent them. We must see it as a starting point, not a finishing line."

She'd nodded in agreement. Sometimes, to stop herself being sick, she would hold her mouth together with her fingers. She did it now, while he talked about personal freedom. He wished she wouldn't.

"True love isn't possessive," he explained to her. "Not our kind of domestic, permanent love. Jealousy, as everyone knows, is a mean and ignoble emotion."

She had agreed and run to the bathroom.

Presently, rather to his dismay, he found the pleasure of sexual experiment enhanced by the knowledge that he would eventually report it to his wife. He stood outside his own body as witness to erotic events. It made the excitement greater and the responsibility less, since he could share it with Ruth.

It was obvious to both of them that it was Ruth's body that was at fault for what she saw as difficulties but which he did not. He had married it perforce and in error and would do his essential duties by it, but he would never be reconciled to its enormity, and Ruth knew it.

Only his parents seemed to expect him to be faithful and kind, as Angus was to Brenda and Brenda to Angus. They treated Bobbo and Ruth as proper husband and wife, not somehow accidentally espoused.

Ruth had wheeled the babies' stroller around the park and taken comfort from licks of their Popsicles and read romantic novels, among them those by Mary Fisher; and Bobbo had gotten on in the world.

Shortly after they had moved into Eden Grove, Bobbo had seen Mary Fisher across a crowded room at his own party and she had seen him and said:

"Let me be your client."

And he had said:

"At once."

And the past paled for Bobbo, including even the agony and ecstasy of Audrey Singer, and the present became all-powerful and the future full of wonderful and dangerous mystery.

This was how the affair began. Bobbo and Ruth gave Mary Fisher a lift home from the party. Mary Fisher had parked her Rolls-Royce impetuously, the sooner to enjoy herself, but unfortunately, for she had obstructed the flow of city traffic, and while she flickered and glittered at her host, the police arrived to tow the vehicle away.

She would, she said, send her manservant Garcia in the morning to retrieve the foolish thing. In the meantime, she said, could Bobbo and Ruth give her a lift back, since they were on her way home?

"Of coourse!" cried Bobbo. "Of course."

Ruth thought that Mary Fisher somehow meant *she* was on *their* way home, but when Bobbo stopped on the corner of Eden Avenue and Nightbird Drive to drop Ruth off, realized her mistake.

"At least take her to the door," protested Mary Fisher, in an act of condescension that Ruth was never to forgive, but Bobbo said, laughing:

"I don't think Ruth is a natural rape victim, somehow. Are you, darling!" and Ruth said, loyally, "I'll be perfectly all right, Miss Fisher. It's just that we live in a dead end and reversing's so difficult in the dark! And we've left the children without a baby-sitter: I really must get back as soon as possible."

But they weren't listening, so she got out of the back—Mary Fisher was in the front, next to Bobbo—and before the door shut heard Mary Fisher say, "You'll never forgive me. I live ever such a way away. Almost to the coast. Actually, on the coast itself," and Bobbo said, "Do you think I didn't know that?" and the door closed and there Ruth was, standing in the dark, while the car zoomed away, and the powerful red rear lights shot off into blackness. Bobbo never drove like that with her: thrum, thrum! And she never caused Bobbo any inconvenience: never asked for a lift here, or an errand there: he always made such a fuss if she did. How did Mary Fisher dare? And why did her presumption charm him, and not offend him? A lift to the *coast* while Ruth would walk in the rain, rather than delay Bobbo fifteen seconds.

She went home and thought about it, lying awake all night, and of course Bobbo did not come home, and in the morning Ruth shouted at the children, and then told herself it wasn't fair to take her distress out on them, and got herself under control, and ate four toasted muffins with apricot jam when the house was quiet and she was alone.

Bobbo came home very tired and missed dinner and went straight to bed and fell asleep and didn't wake until seven the next morning when he said, "Now I know what love is," and got up and dressed, staring at himself in the mirror as if he saw something new there. He was away the next night, and after that two or three nights every week.

Sometimes he'd say he was working late and staying over in town; but sometimes, if he was very tired or very elated, he would confide that he'd been with Mary Fisher, and he'd talk about the dinner guests—famous people, rich people, whom even Ruth had heard of—and what there'd been to eat, and the witty, charming, naughty things Mary Fisher had said, and the dress she'd worn, and what it was like afterward, when at last he could take it off.

33

"Ruth," he'd say, "you're my friend; you must wish me well, in this. Life is so short. Don't begrudge me this experience, this love. I won't leave you; you mustn't worry, you don't deserve to be left; you are the mother of my children: be patient, it will pass. If it hurts you, I'm sorry. But let me share it with you, at least. . . ."

Ruth smiled, and listened, and waited, and it didn't pass. She wondered, in the quiet days, about the nature of women who cared so little for wives.

"One day," she said, "you must take me to dinner at the High Tower. Don't they find it strange that your wife is never there?"

"They're not your sort of people," Bobbo said. "Writers and artists and things like that. And no one who's anyone gets married, these days."

But he must have passed the remark on to Mary Fisher, for presently Ruth was asked to the High Tower. There were only two other guests: the local solicitor and his wife and both elderly. Mary Fisher said the others had canceled at the last moment but Ruth did not believe her.

Bobbo had done his best to stop Mary Fisher issuing an invitation to Ruth, but had failed.

"If she's part of your life, darling," said Mary Fisher, "I want her to be part of mine. I want to meet her properly, not just as someone you discarded on a street corner in the middle of the night. None of my heroines would stand for that! I'll tell you what I'll do. We'll make it one of the duty dinners, not the fun ones."

Sometimes Bobbo asked Mary Fisher why she loved him. Mary Fisher said it was because he was lover and father and what was forbidden and what was allowed all rolled into one, and anyway love was mysterious, and Cupid was willful and why did he want to know, couldn't he just *accept*?

Bobbo did. Ruth came to dinner. She'd tripped and blushed and the hairs on her upper lip and chin caught the light at dinner: she had spilled wine on the tablecloth and said the wrong things to the wrong people, surprising and upsetting things.

"Don't you think," she'd said to the solicitor, "that the more police there are the more crime there is?"

"You mean," he'd said kindly, "the more police, the less crime. Surely."

"No, not surely at all," said Ruth excitedly, spinach quiche slobbering down her chin, and Bobbo had to silence her with a kick under the table.

Sometimes Bobbo thought that Ruth was mad. It wasn't just that she didn't look like other people: she couldn't be relied upon to act like them either.

Bobbo feared that since Mary had properly met Ruth she had cooled a little toward him. It did no one any good to be associated with the unhappy and unfortunate. Love, success, energy, health, happiness went around in a closed circle, self-perpetuating and self-energizing, but precariously balanced. Alter one spoke of the wheel and the whole machine could falter and stop. Good fortune so easily turns to bad! And now he loved Mary Fisher and he loved Mary Fisher and he loved Mary Fisher and his parents had come to dinner and his wife had wept and made a scene, and thrown the dinner about and he did not like her at all. Ruth stood between him and happiness: full square! And in all the history of marriage had there ever been such full-squaredness?

Bobbo had said to Mary Fisher, "Mary, don't you feel guilty about having an affair with a married man?"

And Mary had said, "Is that what we're having, an affair?" and his heart had pounded in terror, until she'd added, "I thought it was more than that. It *feels* like more than that! It feels like forever," so that joy had silenced him, and she'd gone on to say, "Guilty? No. Love is outside our control. We fell in love: it is no one's fault. Not yours. Not mine. And I suppose because Ruth expects nothing, she will never have anything. We can't spoil our lives because she was born with so little joy. You acted out of kindness when you married her, and I love you for it, but now, my love, be kind to me. Live with me. Here, now, forever!"

"And the children?"

"They are Ruth's crown, and her jewels. They are her comfort. She is so lucky. I have no children. I have no one except you."

She said what he wanted to hear. It was entrancing. And now he sat at a suburban table, with his mother, his father, and his past and thought of Mary Fisher, and how she needed him, and longed for a future, and Ruth came in at last with the soup tureen.

Ruth's brave smile faltered over the soup. Her parents-in-law stared up at her in calm and pleasant anticipation. And Ruth gazed at the three dog hairs in that grayish foam that is good mushroom soup, thickened by cream and put through the blender.

The dog's name was Harness. Bobbo had bought him for Andy on Andy's eighth birthday. Ruth looked after him. Harness did not like Ruth. He saw her as a giantess, an affront to the natural order of things. He accepted the food she gave him, but he slept where she told him not to, slunk under cupboards and snapped at searching hands, chewed the upholstery and set up a din if left anywhere he did not want to be. He shed hairs, stole food, ate butter by the pound (when he could find it) and vomited it up directly. Bobbo, on those Sundays he was at home, loved to go walking with Harness in the park, and Andy would go, too, and father and son would feel happy and ordinary and comfortable. Ruth would stay behind, removing dog and cat hairs from fabric of one kind or another with a special vacuum brush, battery powered. She did not like Harness.

"Don't let the soup get cold, Ruth," said Bobbo, as if this were her usual habit.

"Hairs!" was all Ruth said.

"It's a nice clean dog," said Brenda. "We don't mind, do we, Angus?"

"Of course not," said Angus, who did. As a child Bobbo had always wanted a dog, and Angus had always prevented him from having one.

"Can't you even keep the dog out of the soup?" asked Bobbo. It was the wrong thing to say, and he knew it as soon as it was said. He did try not to say "can't you even" to Ruth, but it did slip out whenever he was feeling at odds with her, which of late had been more and more.

Tears appeared in Ruth's eyes. She picked up the soup tureen.

"I'll sieve it," she said.

"What a good idea!" said Brenda. "Then no harm's done."

"Bring the soup back at once," cried Bobbo. "Don't be so silly, Ruth. It isn't a disaster. It's three dog hairs. Just pick them out."

"But they might be the guinea pig's," said Ruth. "He was running along the dresser shelf." She liked the guinea pig least of all the children's pets. Its shoulders were too hunched and its eyes too deep. It reminded her of herself.

"You're tired," said Bobbo. "You must be tired, or you wouldn't talk such nonsense. Sit down."

37

"Let her sieve the soup, dear," said Brenda, "if it's what she wants."

Ruth got as far as the doorway. Then she turned back.

"He doesn't care whether I'm tired or not," Ruth said. "He doesn't think of me anymore. He only ever thinks about Mary Fisher; you know, the writer. She's his mistress."

Bobbo was shocked by this indiscretion, this disloyalty, but also gratified. Ruth was not to be trusted. He'd always known it.

"Ruth," he said, "it's very unfair to my parents to involve them in our family problems. It's nothing to do with them. Have pity, will you, for once, on the helpless bystanders."

"But it *is* something to do with me," said Brenda. "Your father never behaved like that; I don't know where you get it from."

"Kindly respect my privacy, Mother," said Bobbo. "It's the least you can do after the childhood I led."

"And what was the matter with your childhood?" demanded Brenda, turning quite pink.

"Your mother's right," said Angus. "I think you should apologize to her for that. But fair's fair, Brenda, I think you should leave the young people to sort things out in their own way."

"Father," said Bobbo, "it was just that kind of attitude in you that gave me one of the most appalling childhoods any child could have."

Mary Fisher had lately been explaining the roots of his unhappiness to him.

"I never made your mother unhappy," said Angus. "Say what you like about me, but I never deliberately did harm to any woman."

"Then all I can say is," said Brenda, "you did it by accident."

"Women are always imagining things," said Angus.

"Especially Ruth," said Bobbo. "Mary Fisher is one of my best clients. I'm very lucky to have her on my books. I certainly value her both as a creative person—she's remarkably talented —and I like to think as a friend, but I'm afraid our Ruth has a suspicious mind!"

Ruth looked from one parent-in-law to the other and then at her husband and dropped the tureen of mushroom soup, which flowed over the metal rim where the tiles stopped and the carpet began, and the children and the animals returned, summoned by the sound of new disaster. Ruth thought that Harness was laughing.

"Perhaps Ruth ought to get out and get a job," said Angus, on his knees on the floor, spooning soup back into a bowl, but less fast than the carpet absorbed it, so that he had to press the spoon hard into the pile to extract the precious gray liquid. "Keep herself busy: less prone to imagining things."

"There *are* no jobs," Ruth pointed out.

"Nonsense," said Angus. "Anyone who really wants one can get one."

"That's not true," said Brenda. "What with inflation, recession and so on . . . You don't mean us to *eat* that, do you, Angus?"

"Waste not, want not," said Angus.

Bobbo wished to be far, far away, with Mary Fisher, to hear her bubbly laugh, hold her pale hand, and put her little fingers one by one into his mouth until her breathing quickened and she wet her own lips with her pink, pink tongue.

Nicola kicked the cat, whose name was Mercy, out of the way, and the cat went straight to the grate and squatted, crapping its revenge, and Brenda wailed and pointed at Mercy, and Harness became overexcited and leapt up against Andy in semisexual assault, and Ruth just stood there, a giantess, and did nothing, and Bobbo lost his temper.

"See how I have to live!" he shouted. "It's always like this. My wife creates havoc and destruction all around: she destroys everyone's happiness!"

"Why won't you love me?" wailed Ruth.

"How can one love," shouted Bobbo, "what is essentially unlovable?"

"You're both upset," said Angus, giving up the soup to the carpet. "You've been working too hard."

"It's a lot for a woman," said Brenda. "Two growing children! And you were never easy, even as a boy, Bobbo."

"I was perfectly easy," yelled Bobbo. "You just resented every moment you spent on me."

"Come along, Brenda," said Angus. "Least said, soonest mended. We'll eat out."

"A good idea," shouted Bobbo, "since my wife has already thrown your main course on the floor."

"Temper, temper," said Brenda. "In Los Angeles they build houses without kitchens, because nobody bothers to cook. And quite right, too."

"But I spent all day doing this," sobbed Ruth. "And now no one's going to eat it."

"Because it's uneatable!" shouted Bobbo. "Why am I always surrounded by women who can't cook?"

"I'll ring you in the morning, pet," said Brenda to Ruth. "You have a nice bath and get a good night's sleep. You'll feel better then."

"I shall never forgive you for being so rude to my mother," said Bobbo to Ruth, coldly, and loud enough for his mother to hear.

"Don't you go putting the blame on her," said Brenda cunningly. "It was you who was rude, not her. I am a perfectly good cook, I just don't care to do it."

"Marriage isn't easy," remarked Angus, putting on his coat. "It's like parenthood, something people have to work at. Of course, usually it's left to one partner rather than the other."

"It certainly is!" said Brenda meaningfully, drawing on her gloves. She was not focusing properly: she had forgotten to put antiperspirant under her right arm, and her pretty tan blouse was beginning to show a single dark underarm stain. She had a lopsided look.

"Now do you see what's happening?" Bobbo turned on Ruth. "You've even set my parents quarreling! If you see happiness you have to destroy it. It's the kind of woman you are."

Brenda and Angus left. They walked away down the path, side by side but not touching. Domestic strife is catching. Happy couples do well to avoid the company of the unhappy.

Ruth went into the bathroom and locked the door. Andy and Nicola took the chocolate mousse from the fridge and shared it.

"It would serve you right if I went to see Mary," said Bobbo to Ruth, through the keyhole. "You have worked terrible mischief here tonight! You have upset my parents, you have upset your children, and you have upset me. Even the animals were affected. I see you at last as you really are. You are a third-rate person. You are a bad mother, a worse wife, and a dreadful cook. In fact I don't think you are a woman at all. I think that what you are is a she-devil!"

It seemed to him, when he said this, that there was a change in the texture of the silence that came from the other side of the door; he thought perhaps he had shocked her into submission and apology: but though he knocked and banged she still did not come out.

**7** So. I see. I thought I was a good wife tried temporarily and understandably beyond endurance, but no. He says I am a she-devil.

I expect he is right. In fact, since he does so well in the world and I do so badly, I really must assume he is right. I am a she-devil.

But this is wonderful! This is exhilarating! If you are a she-devil, the mind clears at once. The spirits rise. There is no shame, no guilt, no dreary striving to be good. There is only, in the end, what you *want*. And I can take what I want. I am a she-devil!

But what do I want? That of course could be a difficulty. Waverings and hesitations on this particular point can last a whole life long—and for most people usually do. But not, surely, in the case of she-devils. Doubt afflicts the good, not the bad.

I want revenge.
I want power.
I want money.
I want to be loved and not love in return.

I want to give hate its head. I want hate to drive out love, and I want to follow hate where it leads: and then, when I have done what I want with it, and not a minute before, I will master it.

I look at my face in the bathroom mirror. I want to see something different.

I take off my clothes. I stand naked. I look. I want to be changed.

Nothing is impossible, not for she-devils.

Peel away the wife, the mother, find the woman, and there the she-devil is.

Excellent!

Glitter-glitter. Are those my eyes? They're so bright they light up the room.

**8** After Angus and Brenda had gone off into the gathering dusk, their mood of cozy jollity quite broken, and the children had gobbled the last of the chocolate mousse, and the cat Mercy had finished chewing away at the soup-soaked carpet, and Harness the dog had disgorged next door's avocado mousse under the kitchen table, and Ruth was locked in the bathroom, changing her very nature, Bobbo packed his executive suitcase. It was of real red-brown leather with brass trimmings, and unnecessarily heavy.

"Where are you going?" asked Ruth, coming out of the bathroom.

"I am leaving you and going to stay with Mary Fisher," said Bobbo, "until you learn to behave better. I cannot stand all these scenes and sulks about nothing at all."

"How long for?" Ruth asked presently, but Bobbo did not bother to reply. "And why?" she asked. "I mean *really* why?" But she knew what the answer was. Because Mary Fisher was five feet four, self-supporting, childless, had no pets except a cockatoo or so, did not claw the air with desperate hands, and could be taken anywhere without shame. And that was even leaving out the power and mystery of the love that naughty little Mary Fisher inspired in Bobbo's bosom.

"What about me?" asked Ruth, and the words sped out into the universe, to join myriad other "what about me"s uttered by myriad other women, abandoned that very day by their husbands. Women in Korea and Buenos Aires and Stockholm and Detroit and Dubai and Tashkent, but seldom in China, where it is a punishable offense. Sound waves do not die out. They travel forever and forever. All our sentences are immortal. Our useless bleatings circle the universe for all eternity.

"What *about* you?" Bobbo said, to which there is never any answer. "I'll send money back," Bobbo was kind enough to add, packing his shirts. They were ironed so well and folded so neatly he had no trouble in doing so. "You won't really be able to tell the difference whether I'm here or not. You take little or no notice of me when I am here, and of the children none at all."

"The neighbors will be able to tell," Ruth said. "They'll speak to me even less than they do now. They believe misfortune is catching."

"This is not misfortune, exactly," said Bobbo. "Merely the consequence of your actions. Anyway, I'll be back soon, I expect."

She did not think so, for he took his big green canvas suitcase, too; and the ties he wore for special occasions.

Then he went out and Ruth was left alone, standing on the autumn-green carpets between avocado walls, and in the morning the sun rose and slanted through the picture windows and it was obvious that they needed cleaning, and that Ruth was not going to clean them.

"Mom," said Nicola, "the windows are filthy."

"If you don't like them," said Ruth, "you do them."

46

Nicola didn't. Bobbo rang from the office at midday to say he had proposed to Mary Fisher and she had accepted him, so he would not be coming back. He thought Ruth ought to know, so she could make her own plans.

"But—" said Ruth. He rang off. The divorce laws had recently been liberalized so that both parties to the marriage did not have to give their consent to the putting asunder thereof. Just one would do.

"Mom," said Andy, "where's Dad?"

"Gone away," said Ruth, and Andy made no comment. The house was in Bobbo's name. Its purchase had been made possible only by virtue of Angus and Brenda's assistance, after all. Ruth had come to the marriage with nothing. Except size, and strength, and those she still had.

"Where's dinner?" Nicola asked presently, but there was none. So she spread peanut butter onto sliced bread, and handed it around. She used the bread knife to get the peanut butter out of the jar, and cut her finger, and threads of blood laced the finished slice. But no one remarked upon it.

They ate silently.

Nicola, Andy, and Ruth consumed their food sitting in front of the television. So little groups eat, women and children, when the world falls apart.

Presently Ruth muttered something.

"What did you say?" asked Nicola.

"Dumped," said Ruth. "That's what happens to the plain and virtuous. They get dumped."

Nicola and Andy rolled their eyes and looked to heaven. They thought she was mad. Their father had said so often enough. "Your mother's mad," he'd say.

In the morning Nicola and Andy went to school.

Some days later Bobbo telephoned to say that he would allow Ruth and the children to go on living in the house in the meanwhile, although the place was obviously too big for them. They'd be happier in something much smaller.

"In the meanwhile till what?" she asked, but he did not reply. He said he would pay her $52 a week until further notice, which was twenty percent above the legal minimum. Thanks to the new legislation which gave second wives a fairer deal, he was required to support only his children. Able-bodied first wives were expected to stand on their own feet.

"Ruth," said Bobbo, "you have very good, very solid feet. You'll be okay."

"But it costs at least one hundred and sixty-five dollars a week to run the house," said Ruth.

"That's why it will have to be sold," said Bobbo. "But do bear in mind that when I'm not there costs will come right down. Women and children don't consume nearly as much as men; statistics prove it. Besides, now the children are at school, in fact nearly grown-up, it's time you went back to work. It's not good for a woman to molder away at home."

"But the children will be ill; school holidays are half the year; and besides, there *are* no jobs."

"There is always work for those who want it," said Bobbo. "Everyone knows that."

He was telephoning from the High Tower. In a corner of the great room Mary Fisher bowed her pretty neck and wrote sweet words about the nature of love.

"His fingers moved suddenly and she felt their tips trail provocatively across her skin to the trembling softness of her mouth," wrote Mary Fisher, and Bobbo put down the telephone and she put down her pen, and they kissed, and sealed their future together.

**9** Mary Fisher lives in the High Tower with my husband, Bobbo, and writes about the nature of love, and sees no reason why everyone should not be happy.

Why should she think about us? We are powerless, and poor, and have no importance. We are not even included in everyone.

I daresay Bobbo sometimes wakes in the night, and she asks what is the matter, and he says, "I am thinking about the children," and she says, "Better the way you did it, making a clean break, not seeing them," and he believes her, because Andy and Nicola are not the kind of children to tug anyone's heartstrings, let alone someone whose hairy legs are entwined with Mary Fisher's little silky ones.

And if he ever says, "I wonder how Ruth's getting on," she will stop his mouth with a morsel of smoked salmon, a sip of champagne, and say, "Ruth will make her own way in the world. After all, she has the children. Poor me, I have none! All I have is you, Bobbo."

My two children come and go, sucking sustenance, nuzzling away, but I have nothing to give them. How can I? She-devils have dry dugs. It takes a little time to become wholly she-devil. One feels positively exhausted at first, I can tell you. The roots of self-reproach and good behavior tangle deep in the living flesh: you can't ease them out gently; they have to be torn out, and they bring flesh with them.

Sometimes in the night I scream so loud I wake the neighbors. Nothing ever wakes the children.

In the end I sucked energy out of the earth. I went into the garden and turned the soil with a fork, and power moved into my toes and up my stubborn calves and rested in my she-devil loins: an urge and an irritation. It said there must now be an end to waiting: the time for action has come.

**10** Carver lived in a hut down at the Eden Grove athletic field where he was caretaker. He was over sixty, whiskery and wrinkled, but bright eyed. The skin of his arms was red and tough, but where it stretched over his belly it was white, thin, and taut. The hut stood where the tennis courts and the running track met, and was where Carver was meant to keep mowers and rollers, and exercise his supervisory duties by day: but now he stayed there by night as well, lying on a foam-rubber mattress under a dirty blanket, sometimes sleeping, more often not. He was an employee of the local authority—half a charity, half useful. He reported bee swarms and chased off children and courting couples.

Carver was reputed to have suffered brain damage when rescuing a child from drowning on some faraway beach. For this reason the ladies of Eden Grove, when presenting their petition to have him replaced, asked for his early retirement rather than immediate removal and formal disgrace. Wives and mothers had to pass the sports field on the way to shops and school and had to hurry past, eyes averted. Sometimes Carver merely leered: sometimes he exposed himself. Though no one had actually seen this happen, everyone knew someone who had.

Carver watched Ruth coming down the road. He liked the flash of her dark eyes; he enjoyed her lumbering gait. She did not trit-trot, as did other wives and mothers, on little heels. Her shoes were flat, perhaps because her feet were too large to fit into anything elaborate. Carver knew well enough that one day she would come in for a cup of tea. He knew in advance who would be intimately associated with him, and that all he had to do—all anyone had to do—having recognized a future partner, was to wait. Love, he had always known, was nothing but fore-knowledge of either happiness or pain.

Carver knew how to want, but not want too much; he knew how to hope, but not too fiercely; how to wait, but not for too long. Carver liked to drift along on the current of fate, with an easy turn here and an easy turn there, a casual twist of will and hope, a fish in the flowing stream of time.

"Come in and have a cup of tea," he said, standing close to the tennis-court fence as she passed by. She came in.

Ruth drank her tea from a cracked mug. An iron wood stove burned at the end of the hut, although it was summer. They sat close together in front of it, as though it were winter. News-papers made a carpet on the floor. They sat so close they touched. She would have made two of him but it didn't seem to matter. Her eyes glittered. He remarked upon it.

"They glitter when I know what I want," she said.

"What is it you want?"

It would be money or sex, he knew, they being the two most important things in life.

"You," she said. His arm slid around her shoulder. His face descended into a series of skinny chins. Eyes heavy with age stared into hers. He understood a certain kind of woman, had entertained more than enough of them, in his time, in his shed at the end of the tennis courts. Good, suburban wives, neatly dressed and properly washed, seeking something beyond degra-dation so that it approached mysticism, trit-trotting into his shed. Men and women, in unsanctioned and temporary love, leaping and wriggling through the rivers of time. Nothing wrong there. This one was different: she had another reason. He did not understand it.

She had hairs sprouting from moles beneath her chin. Well, he had hairs that grew out of his nostrils. Her breasts were like cushions. He laid his old head upon them. She smiled. He had no worries about his sexual performance. Erections were a young man's preoccupation; fingers and hands would do as well for her, if necessary. But when it came to it he trembled and wept, the invited guest barred at the door by his own guilt: kept in the cold when all was warm and soft inside.

"I can't," he said. "Something's wrong. Why did you come here?"

"This was the first step," she said. "The breaking of the first rule."

"What rule's that?" He knew about rules. There was a bulletin board covered with them at every entrance to the field. Carver found it difficult to read. Once he could; now he couldn't.

"Discrimination." She had a low laugh; he liked it, and did better.

Carver had a vision: Carver soared out the other side of tumultuous clouds, into space. Carver saw Ruth standing in the middle of a different universe, naked and honey-limbed, and around her danced new slow-rhythmed stars. He was mouthing away at her source, he understood; he was burying his head in flesh, and it was scented not with the natural juices of creation but with existence itself. He was not strong enough for it. He was made for the old world, not the new.

He was a poor old man; he trembled with love and lust; his eyes turned up, whitely, electrical discharges crackled through his brain, feebling it as they always had, from the beginning. Visions wear out old flesh. He was on his knees. He fell.

Ruth looked with amazement at the body on the floor. Carver was having a fit, and she was sorry, but could do little about it.

Ruth was pleased with herself. She and this writhing senior citizen had between them constructed a crisscross base on which the new foundations of her life would stand, as upholstery stands upon its webbing. The webs were pain and pleasure, humiliation and exultation, transfiguration and degradation, properly accepted: the construction would take amazing weight, amazing strains. There were little gaps still, here and there, through which she might slip. She would have to be careful.

The foaming and the jerking stopped. Carver lay in the warmth of his excrement, quietly asleep. Ruth took the cigarettes from the open packet on the table, put them in her coat pocket, and left, and walked down toward High Street for more peanut butter, some multipoint adaptors, and to order a taxi for the morning; a large plain woman in sensible shoes, holding a shopping basket, expected to be grateful for what she had.

Well! Who has Mary Fisher slept with, in the High Tower? Probably not many. She is too fastidious. Certainly not the gardener, or his fingers would be greener, his pay envelope larger.

Perhaps in the past a millionaire or two, or a publisher or so, to help her get by. They will have laid their graying, powerful heads next to hers, upon the pale goosedown pillows.

Garcia is a different matter. I think he does for her when the night is dark and lonely, or the creative flow dries up, and the sentences stumble and falter beneath her pen. Then I think he slides into her bed and into her. When I fell over the rug I saw understanding flash between the two of them, a joint complicity. Bobbo first, but Garcia next. Bobbo won't like that.

I wish impotence upon Bobbo, and Garcia, and the gardener because he can't keep even such a simple tree as a poplar growing straight and strong. Like master, like tree: perhaps there's no need to wish it.

I wish thrush on Mary Fisher, just to start with. Perhaps I can feed a Monilia brew into the central heating system, and puff it out everywhere, so that when she lies entwined with Bobbo on the long white sofa it's all about, waiting. Let her suppurate; let her rot. I have experienced sex with only two men: Bobbo and

Carver. I preferred Carver. Bobbo stole my strength from me, but I stole Carver's.

I am frightened. I belong nowhere, neither to the ranks of the respectable nor the damned. Even whores, these days, must be beautiful. As a woman my physical match is an old, epileptic, half-witted man. And I accept it, and in the accepting have lost my place, my chair at the edge of the great ballroom where the million, million wallflowers sit, and have done since the beginning of time, watching and admiring, never joining the dance, never making claims, avoiding humiliation, but always hoping.

One day, we vaguely know, a knight in shining armor will gallop by, and see through to the beauty of the soul, and gather the damsel up and set a crown on her head, and she will be queen.

But there is no beauty in my soul, not now, and I have no place, so I must make my own, and since I cannot change the world, I will change myself.

I am invigorated. Self-knowledge and reason run through my veins: the cold slow blood of the she-devil.

**12** On Saturday morning Ruth prepared a proper break-fast for Andy and Nicola. She used up all the eggs that should have lasted through until Thursday—the day that the fresh egg deliveries were made at the local shop—and all the bacon in the house. She found white sliced bread in the bottom of the freezer—since Bobbo's departure its level had sunk lower and lower—and made toast. She put butter on the table instead of margarine and required the children to finish a whole half pot of honey. They looked at her with wary eyes, and ate.

Ruth herself had lost her appetite. She drank fresh black coffee, made from beans scraped up from the furry ice that lined the bottom of the freezer.

She gave Harness a whole pound of butter to eat, and did not follow him through the house to see where he vomited. She imagined it would be beneath the double bed, where she so often lay alone. She had left the bedroom door open, which normally, for fear of Harness and Mercy, she never did. She gave Mercy two complete cans of sardines, meant for human consumption.

She gave Richard the guinea pig nothing. He had chewed too many holes into the chests of too many woollen sweaters, and she could find no remnant of concern for him left in her. Why should Richard have treats, when she had none?

After breakfast Ruth left the dishes where they were and told the children to search the house for money. They looked under the edges of carpets and the crack where the oven met the fridge, in the nutty sludge at the bottom of their toy boxes and behind the books on their shelves, between the piles of child art at the top of cupboards and at the back of wardrobes and, of course, down the clefts of sofas and chairs. They found coins to the value of $6.23.

"Now," said Ruth, "you will go to MacDonald's and buy what you want: Big Macs, Super Macs, Slice O'Fish, apple pie, and as many milk shakes as you want, on condition that you return here at exactly eleven A.M. No earlier, no later."

"It's not enough," said Nicola.

"It's all I have," said Ruth. "I have given you everything I have to give, remember that. And all I ever had was scraps and leavings."

They did not understand or care, and went off to MacDonald's complaining.

The summer had been long and hot. Already the sun was well up, taking what little moisture the night had left. But there was a good breeze.

Ruth went through the house as a good housewife should in such weather, and opened all the windows. She went into the kitchen and poured a whole bottle of oil into the deep fryer, so that it brimmed, and lit a low gas flame beneath it. She estimated that it would take some twenty minutes for the oil to reach the boiling point. She adjusted the kitchen curtains so that they hung as the architect had intended, cheek by jowl with the stove. She plugged in all the electrical appliances in the house—except the lamps, which might attract neighborly attention—using multipoint adaptors bought especially for this purpose.

Dishwasher, washing machine, dryer, exhaust fan, air conditioner, three television sets, four electronic games, two convection heaters, a hi-fi system, sewing machine, vacuum cleaner, blender, three electric blankets (one very old), and the steam iron. She set them all to maximum performance and turned on all the switches. The house roared, and presently a slight smell of burning rubber filled the air. Such sounds and smells were not unusual in Eden Grove on a Saturday morning; just rather more intense than normal, as they wafted over Nightbird Drive.

Ruth went back into the kitchen and turned on the gas in the oven, then knelt and pushed down the plunger that worked an electric spark. This plunger, if held down for at least some nine or ten seconds, heated to red-hot a metal flange, which then ignited the gas in the oven. It had always been an annoying device. This morning she held the plunger down for only eight seconds. Then she removed her finger and closed the oven door without checking that the flame had lit.

She went into Andy's room. He had been drawing and there were some sixty sheets of paper on the floor, and some thirty felt-tipped pens, mostly without tops. She dragged his beanbag, filled with polystyrene foam, to a point just in front of the electric fire he loved to put on just before going to sleep on chilly nights. The walls were lined with posters and pennants.

She went into Nicola's room and saw that it was not only strewn with candy wrappers but that Nicola had been trying to make three feather pillows out of one torn comforter. She knocked over a bottle of turpentine that Nicola had failed to seal.

Bobbo's study, at the back of the house, into which the neighbors could not so easily see, was littered with papers. Ruth had been going through the drawers, sorting out her possessions and his, dividing their lives. Two large wastepaper baskets were more than full and there were two bags made of black plastic— the kind that is cheap but tears easily—stuffed with outdated documents, bills, and letters, leaning against the desk, waiting to be put out of the house. Ruth drew the curtains to keep the sun out, sat down at Bobbo's desk, and smoked one of the cigarettes she had taken from Carver's table. She did it inexpertly, not normally being a smoker, and did not much care for it, and when she had taken a puff or so, she stubbed the cigarette out and threw it into the wastepaper basket at the foot of the curtains. She stubbed it out carelessly, and it smoldered. How could a nonsmoker know? Most fires, when extinguished, go out and stay out.

Then Ruth left the room, leaving the door open. A cool draft blew through. She went back to the kitchen, where the oil was beginning to bubble and, after a little thought, called forgivingly to Harness and Mercy, who were so startled by this attention that Harness took refuge beneath the double bed in the master bedroom and Mercy leaked away on top of it, in her usual mixture of vengeance and fright.

Ruth ignored nips and scratches and removed both animals from the house. She forgot the guinea pig. He had earned forgetfulness. She dragged the double mattress off the bed, heaved it over the bedroom balcony railings and down into the side garden, which her neighbor, Rosemary, overlooked.

Ruth began to hose down the mattress. Rosemary from next door looked over the low fence. Her hair was in rollers.

"What are you doing, Ruth?" she asked.

"It's the animals," said Ruth. "It's either do this or buy a new mattress. You know what cats are!"

"Not if they're neutered," said Rosemary, and went back inside.

She reappeared presently, saying, "Can you smell burning?"

"No," said Ruth. "If anything's smelling it's this mattress."

Rosemary went back in, to reappear shortly.

"Are you sure there's not some kind of fire?" she said. "Isn't that smoke at the back of the house?"

"Good God," said Ruth, "I think you're right."

At that moment the kitchen exploded. It was ten in the morning, exactly. The two women ran to call the fire department and the police from the telephone in Rosemary's house.

"Thank God the children are out!" said Rosemary. "Where are they?"

"At MacDonald's," said Ruth, and Rosemary, even at such a moment, tut-tutted.

Ruth wept and wailed and clung to her neighbor, and the black fumes from burning polystyrene prevented the firemen from rescuing Richard the guinea pig in time. The limp body was brought out, extracted too late from smoldering hay.

"He didn't suffer," said a fireman. "The smoke got him first."

"But I loved him, I loved him," cried Ruth, and the chief of police thought, Poor giant lady, she had to love something, and now she has nothing.

"They shouldn't allow these new foam chips," said the fireman. "It happens all the time. One minute a home's there, the next it isn't."

The fact seemed to gratify them. Their hoses merely seemed to exacerbate matters. Smoke clouds billowed over Eden Grove, blotting out the sunlight in Nightbird Drive. Neighbors, many in curlers, gathered and clung and whispered.

"It never rains but it pours," they said. "Poor Ruth, what will she do? No husband, no home, and the guinea pig dead!"

But in their hearts they were glad she was going. She had never really fitted in. When she had given lunches something had always gone wrong, and Andy looked up the skirts of the little girls, and Nicola was rumored to steal. The neighbors offered tea to the firemen, who took off their boots and helmets and sat their smoky handsome selves on pale polystyrene sofas, and if children and husbands were out, in one or two instances nipped up to the bedrooms. Fire and danger and disaster are great aphrodisiacs.

"So you're the lady of the house," said the insurance man. He arrived at ten fifty-five to view the scene and assess responsibility and blame. He had been notified of the fire by the police. They reported all house fires on the spot. There had been too many of them lately.

"I was," said Ruth, brave through her tears.

"That's the spirit! Remember, we're here to help you. A write-off, I should say. But no lives lost, that's the main thing."

"There was the guinea pig," lamented Ruth.

"We'll help you buy another," he said. "Or at any rate sixty percent of another. Unless of course there was negligence. I took a quick look at your file before I came down." He offered her a cigarette.

"Do you smoke?"

She accepted it.

"Thank you. I've smoked a lot since my husband left. You know how it is. Nerves."

"Perhaps that's how it started? A cigarette in a wastepaper basket? Not properly stubbed out? It's so easy."

"It might have been," said Ruth. "In fact, now I come to think of it, I was sorting papers in Bobbo's room, and started crying — Oh!" She clapped her hand over her mouth. "What have I said?"

"The truth is always best," he said, busily writing.

"Oh, no, no!" wailed Ruth. "Whatever will poor Bobbo say?"

At eleven o'clock Andy and Nicola arrived, pleased with their second breakfast and their punctuality, and the taxi turned up as well, and Ruth, carrying a black plastic bag of rescued belongings, pushed the children into the back, and got in the front beside the driver. He feared her large thighs would get in the way of the hand brake. She was a strange sight—her face smoke-blackened and her eyes glittering.

"We're going to the coast," she told the children. "We're going to see Daddy."

The driver surveyed the dark shell of her once-lovely home. "Was that yours?" he asked, awed. The children were crying in the back, but were so full of hamburgers their distress was more token than anything else, and trauma on the whole was averted, which was what she had anticipated.

"Let's just get away," Ruth begged. "It does the children no good to look at a scene like that. The end of the life they've known."

He accelerated obligingly. Ruth looked back when the taxi reached the top of the hill and saw No. 19 Nightbird Drive as a lost tooth, a black and empty socket, in an otherwise gleaming, smiling mouth and was glad.

"What about Harness, what about Mercy?" wept the children. They did not mention the guinea pig, and she did not remind them.

"They're alive," said Ruth, "and I'm sure the neighbors will look after them; they're so fond of animals!"

"Our books, our toys!" they wept.

"Gone, all gone," she said. "But I'm sure your father will buy you more."

"Are we going to live with him?"

"You have nowhere else to live, my dears."

"You, too?"

"No," said Ruth. "Your father lives with someone else now, and there's no changing that. But I'm sure she'll be happy to have you, she loves him so much."

**13** Mary Fisher lives in the High Tower. She loves it there. Was there ever a more enchanting address? High Tower, the Old Lighthouse, World's End? When Mary Fisher bought the place five years ago it was a ruin. Now it is the outer and visible sign of her achievement. She loves the way the evening sun stretches across the sea onto the old stone and makes everything a warm soft pinky yellow. Who needs rose-tinted glasses when reality is so cozy? It can be done, you see. Mary Fisher has done it.

It is dangerous to love houses, to put your trust in buildings.

Who needs a knight in shining armor when Bobbo is there, in his beautifully laundered shirt, in his well-cut, fine-seamed suit, made in best, in softest mohair, and full of adoration, admiration? Mary Fisher has made her books come true. It can be done. She's done it.

It is dangerous to love men, to put your trust in love.

It is even more dangerous to have house and man in the same basket.

I could have told Mary Fisher that but she didn't ask me. Besides, she-devils do not offer advice. Why should they?

The flames were wonderful. They warmed my chilly blood.

**14** Garcia enjoyed working at the High Tower. He had personal charm, physical strength, and an easy nature and was well suited to his work. He alone could keep in order the Dobermans that guarded Mary Fisher's property: they loped at his heels and so he had no trouble in keeping the rest of the staff—two maids, a cook, and a gardener—in order, too. Garcia had his own room, with a sea view, which was warm in winter and cool in summer. He was young and healthy. He sent his wages home to his mother in Spain; he did not know that she had married again. In his spare time he would go down to the village and drink. There were three young village women and two young fishermen all in love with him, and because he could talk fast and convincingly and had great sexual energy, none of them minded too much about the existence of the others. If any man could be deemed happy that man was Garcia.

Garcia admired Mary Fisher for her style, her looks, her wealth. He thought she was placed above him as the shiny moon is above the dark earth, there where nature had ordained. During the four years of his employment he had made love to her on five occasions. He saw it as only right that he should serve her needs, tactfully and unobtrusively. If she cried in the night he would go to her, and in the morning they would be mistress and manservant again, formal as ever.

Others of her lovers came and went, all richer, grander, and more powerful than he, and he did not resent them. How could he? Their rights in the world were greater than his. The rich man in his castle, the poor man at his gate, and so forth. And she needed her lovers—as indeed she needed him, Garcia, for her work, for her writing. How was Mary Fisher to describe the tremors of the flesh, the yearnings of the heart, if she did not feel them? They are so soon forgotten, just like the pangs of childbirth.

When Bobbo arrived with his two suitcases Garcia was at first merely disconcerted. When Mary Fisher welcomed Bobbo in, became pink and tremulous and fluttery with pleasure, and made room for his clothes in her closet, Garcia was displeased. He had assumed that were Mary Fisher ever to join her life to another's it would be to someone even richer and grander than she. She would cease to be the moon—she would become the sun. Bobbo, Garcia had always felt, was only a cut above a servant himself; an adviser, a professional. A city man who knew nothing of the sea or of coastal life; who walked on the edges of the cliffs to show that he was brave and strolled at the sea's edge in a storm to show who was master, and who did not understand what salt did to glass, or wood or human flesh, and ordered the windows opened in a high wind, the better to feel the force and glory of nature. Not only did he lack power, he lacked wisdom. Garcia sulked and sent a maid up with the early morning tea.

When Garcia saw the taxi come up the drive of the High Tower and Ruth and the children get out, he was gratified. Ruth, he knew, meant trouble. She had come to dinner once, and torn a hole in a valuable rug and spilled red wine on a white Portuguese lace cloth, leaving a stain that not even professional cleaning could remove.

Mary Fisher was in the studio with Bobbo when the taxi arrived. Garcia took it upon himself to ring through on the internal telephone but neither Mary nor Bobbo answered. They were, he assumed, too busy making love to answer. He felt angry, dispossessed and restless, like a rooster in the farmyard when one of the hens prefers the second-in-command.

Ruth rang the bell on the great oak door. The Dobermans leapt up against it, barking, shaking the massive boards. He heard the sound of wailing, frightened children. He restrained the dogs and opened the door.

"I have come to see my husband," said Ruth above the uproar. "And the children have come to see their father."

She stood upon the steps like a figure carved in stone: a giant chess piece, a clumsy black rook come to challenge the little white ivory queen. The dogs whined and fell silent. Garcia thought she had the same expression in her eyes, a reddish glitter, as his mother had on the day she'd flung his drunken father out, risking murder at his hand. He crossed himself. Ruth smelled slightly of smoke, which made him think of hell-fire. He stood aside to let her pass. He was both frightened and challenged by her. Garcia of the five compliant lovers, three female, two male, thought he could dice with the Devil if he wanted. And why not? All a man had to do with fear was outface it.

"Where are they?" she asked, and Garcia pointed upward. He saw no reason to save Bobbo and Mary from the consequences of their actions. Ruth nodded and went up the circular stone stairway that was the center of the house. The stairs were wide and low—the cold indoor stone warmly carpeted in pink. The children toiled up behind her, complaining because there was no lift. Ruth moved her large bulk upward, around and around, with surprising ease. Garcia, following on behind, thought perhaps he could manage her: she would be his three girlfriends rolled into one. He could reduce the loving courtship rituals the village girls demanded by two-thirds and still find satisfaction. The term *bulk buy* came into his mind.

Ruth reached the top landing of the lighthouse. Mary Fisher's great studio room spread itself out beneath cantilevered oak beams. The wood was old, hard and seasoned by salt water. Once these beams had formed the backbones of Elizabethan battleships, men o'war; or so the architect had said. The cost of the conversion from lighthouse to dwelling had been some $250,000 and had provided employment for many, locally and from afar. Ruth knew this: she was familiar with Mary Fisher's accounts. Bobbo had spent a lot of time with them at Nightbird Drive, as if he could not get enough of them at the office but had to bring them home.

Mary Fisher and Bobbo were in the act of love on the white sofa, as Garcia had assumed they would be, when Ruth interrupted their pleasure.

Bobbo wore his best white silk shirt and gray jacket and nothing else. Mary Fisher wore nothing. She made little mewing sounds of pleasure, but hardly, Garcia thought, loud enough to drown out the sound of the telephone. If they did not choose to answer it, they had no one to blame except themselves for what happened next. Bobbo and Mary Fisher did not at first notice Ruth's presence, or the children's; when they did it was Bobbo who wished to stop and Mary Fisher who wished to continue.

Andy and Nicola stood with their mouths open. Their mother did nothing to spare them the sight of their father's lanky, passionate half nakedness as he disengaged himself from Mary Fisher.

"Take the children out of here," said Bobbo sharply, pulling on his trousers, forgetting his underpants. "This is no place for them."

"It is the only place," said Ruth, "they will ever get to view the primal scene."

"Poor Bobbo," said Mary Fisher. "I see what you mean. She is intolerable." She pulled a yellow fringed shawl around her shoulders and belted its fronds around her waist with a pink silk cord, so it hung like a dress of the most expensive kind, through which glimpses of delectable flesh could occasionally be seen.

"Garcia," said Mary Fisher, "you really should have prevented this intrusion."

"I'm sorry, ma'am," said Garcia, averting his eyes, as if his mistress's nakedness were unknown to him. "There was no stopping her."

"I imagine there seldom is," said Mary forgivingly.

"Nicola and Andy," said Ruth, "you are in a very wonderful and interesting place. It is a converted lighthouse. That is why there are so many stairs. And this is a very famous, very rich lady, who writes books. Her name is Mrs. Fisher and your father loves her very much, and you must love her, too, for his sake."

"Miss Fisher," corrected Mary Fisher.

"I'm sure you will love being here," Ruth went on. "Look! You can see seagulls outside the windows and if you look down there's a swimming pool carved into the rocks below. Isn't that wonderful?"

"Is it heated?" asked Nicola.

"I can't look down," said Andy. "Heights make me feel sick."

"Then look over here, Andy; there's a cocktail bar carved right into the old stone wall. Lot of mixers and peanuts and crisps, too. You'll love those. I'm sure Mrs. Fisher will get in orange juice as soon as she can. Won't she, Bobbo?"

Bobbo stood between his two children as if he felt he ought to defend them, but was not quite sure against what.

"Garcia," said Mary Fisher, "I think this lady is simply upset. Take the children down to the kitchen, please. Feed them, or whatever it is that people do with children."

"They are not bears, Mary," said Bobbo, "to be fed with buns." Mary Fisher looked as if she doubted this.

"Ruth," said Bobbo, "please take the children home. If you want to talk to me, I'll meet you for lunch somewhere in town. But really there is nothing for us to discuss."

"I can't go home," said Ruth.

"You must," said Mary, little lips pouting. "You simply have not been invited here. You are trespassing. I have dogs, you know. I could set them against you, if I so wished. Intruders have no protection in law. Isn't that so, Garcia?"

"Ma'am," said Garcia, "I wouldn't advise setting the dogs on anyone. Not Dobermans. Enemies today, you and me tomorrow. It's the taste of blood, like sharks."

"Even so," said Mary Fisher.

"Mary," said Bobbo. "There is no point in getting upset. It is obvious that the children can't stay here. They must go home where they belong, with their mother."

"Why is it obvious?" asked Ruth. Nicola was helping herself to peanuts at the bar and Andy had turned on the little portable TV, rather loud. They knew they would be advised when some decision as to their future had been reached. In the meantime they found the discussion both painful and boring.

"Because I'm simply so bad with children," said Mary Fisher. "Look at me. Do I seem the maternal type? Besides, if I ever had children they would most certainly be my own. Wouldn't they, Bobbo?"

She looked lovingly up at Bobbo and he looked lovingly down, and both envisaged their mutual children, as unlike Andy and Nicola as could possibly be.

"And what is more," Mary Fisher went on, "this house is simply no good for children. There are so few doors and so many stairwells to fall down, and the dogs are snappy. Isn't that so, Garcia? The best place for them is with you, Ruth, in their own home, with their own mother. Of course Bobbo should visit them, eventually, and he means to do so as soon as you have calmed down, but you know how he dreads scenes. And it wouldn't be good for Andy and Nicola to see you two at loggerheads. We have to think of them."

"As soon as you are in a smaller house, Ruth," said Bobbo, "you'll feel better. There'll be less work. You won't be tired and depressed all the time. And I'm not insensitive. I do understand that living in Nightbird Drive, with all the memories it holds for you, of life with me, must be upsetting for you. The sooner it's sold, the better."

"I'm glad we've had this talk," said Mary Fisher. "It clears the air. Bobbo needs all the capital he can raise. We want to build an office for him here: a cantilevered extension. I know the tower looks large, but it's simply amazing how small it really is. With all the advances in information technology in recent years he can all but run his practice from here, and need only go to the town office twice a week. We don't want to hurry you, Ruth, but the sooner the house is sold the better. Bobbo wants to pay his way: he simply doesn't want to have to feel indebted to me; I'm sure you understand that."

"The thing is, Mary," said Ruth, "there simply isn't a house to sell. It burned down this morning. And there simply isn't a home for me to take the children back to, unless we burrow in the ashes, so they'll have to stay here."

When Bobbo had finished blaming Ruth for her carelessness, and Mary Fisher had telephoned the police and the fire department to verify Ruth's story, and Andy and Nicola had realized that the guinea pig was dead, and the noise had died down, except for an occasional asthmatic gasp from Bobbo, Mary Fisher said, "I suppose that in the circumstances the children had better stay, for just a day or two, while we work something more sensible out. Garcia, will you drive Mrs. Patchett to the station? She must have had such a tiring day. She can just catch the evening train, if she goes now."

And she left the room, her little white behind twinkling through the yellow fronds, her part in the conversation clearly at an end. But not before she'd caught a glimpse of Nicola's casual heel grinding crisps into the Persian rug, and Andy spurting Coca-Cola from his mouth all over the whitewashed walls, as he accidentally sneezed.

Ruth prepared to go.

"But what about their things?" asked Bobbo, following after her. "Where are their things? Trainers and underpants and jerseys and toys and coloring pencils and so on."

"All gone. Burned. Buy some more."

"I'm not made of money. And it's Saturday, and the shops are closed, and it's Sunday tomorrow."

"It very often is," said Ruth. "Just when you want something you find the shops are closed."

"And what about their school, Ruth? They're going to miss school."

"Find them another."

"There *are* no schools around here."

"There are always schools for those who want them," said Ruth.

"But where are you going?" he demanded. "To friends?"

"What friends?" she inquired. "But I'll stay here, if you want."

"You know that's out of the question."

"Then I'll go."

"But you'll leave an address?"

"No," said Ruth, "I don't have one."

"But you can't just desert your own children!"

"I can," said Ruth.

Garcia escorted Ruth to the front door. The Dobermans panted after her. She exuded some new scent: of triumph, freedom, and fear, all mixed. They found it heady. Their noses ruffled up under her sage-green smock.

"The dogs have good taste," said Garcia. He sat her in the back of the Rolls-Royce. "Which way are you going?" he asked. "East or west? Platform one or two?"

"Either will do," she said. "Just put me on a train."

He understood that she was crying. He looked over his shoulder and saw her large shoulders shaking.

"It had to be done," she said. "There was nothing else to do. It was them or me."

"I'll keep an eye on them," said Garcia, and meant it. "Anytime you want to telephone, I'll let you know what's going on."

"Thank you, Garcia."

"Do you want him back?" he asked. He supposed she would. Men have trouble believing that women can ever do without them.

"Yes," said Ruth, "but on my own terms."

"What are they?"

"They're rather special," was all she'd say.

She took the eastbound train; a very tall, very large lady with a dirty face and red-rimmed eyes, wearing a sage-green tentlike dress and carrying a black garbage bag full of personal belongings hitched over one shoulder.

"Why does that woman look so funny?" asked a little boy, who sat opposite Ruth in the train.

"Hush, hush!" said the mother, and took him to sit somewhere else.

**15** Mary Fisher has built her tower around her, and cemented the stone with bank notes, and lined the walls inside with stolen love, but still she is not safe. She has a mother.

Old Mrs. Fisher lives in a house for the elderly. I know, because a monthly payment goes to the matron, and there is a question as to whether the extras (one bottle of sherry a week, four packages of chocolate-chip cookies) are tax-deductible. The file is thick. Bobbo is good at detail. So is Mary Fisher. Bobbo moves his tongue over Mary Fisher's left nipple, quickly, from right to left, and she gives a little gasp of pleasure.

But I need a little time. Soon I will mend but now I hurt. The she-devil is wounded: she has slunk back into her lair: the ogre motherhood paces outside with heavy feet.

I must think of this grief as a physical pain. I must remember that just as a broken leg heals with time so with this psychic injury. There will be no disfiguring scar tissue: this is an inner wound, not an outer one.

I am a woman learning to be without her children. I am a snake shedding its skin. It makes no difference that the children are Nicola and Andy, that they lack charm. A child is a child: a mother, a moth. I twist and squirm with guilt and pain, even knowing that the quieter I stay the quicker I will heal, slip the old skin, and slither off renewed into the world.

I'm sure I miss them more than they miss me. They have been the meaning of my life: I have merely served their growing purposes, as old Mrs. Fisher once served her daughter Mary.

**16** Geoffrey Tufton came to this particular TraveLodge three times a year, and went from firm to firm in the city, promoting new advances in information technology. Once he had flown from country to country doing the same thing but on a grander scale, dealing with orders worth tens of thousands, even hundreds of thousands of dollars. But something had happened—his personality had not fitted, or he had failed to clinch a deal just once too often—or perhaps it was his wife's refusal to blend, to enter into the company spirit; he could not be sure—and the air trips became fewer and the train trips more frequent, and promotion did not come, and inflation overtook his salary and these days he was glad enough of the TraveLodge, and the drinks at the bar he could acquire on his expense account.

It was his fifty-first birthday and he had no one with whom to celebrate—if such a day merited celebration. He had weighed himself and discovered he was a full fifteen pounds heavier than he thought. Worse, he had a stubborn conjunctivitis in one eye: it itched, it wept, it drizzled pus. His doctor had suggested the ailment was psychosomatic in origin, which made him yet more miserable. He was unsightly, overweight, and useless. He kept his bad eye to the wall, in the corner of the bar, and drank, and watched his fellow salesmen pick up the girls who came in, discreet night visitors, and knew he had no chance with them at all. His eye smacked of disease. They thought nothing of age or paunchiness, except to put their prices up, but were nervous of skin eruptions, inflamed eyes, or sores around the mouth. And why not? He was half-glad, because he did not like deceiving his wife, although she was to blame for many of his troubles, but only *half* because she lately had taken a job of her own, all but outearning him, and depriving him of his sense of purpose, his reward for the life he led—that is, the thought that he supported her.

He watched Ruth come into the bar. She had to bend her neck to pass through the mock-Tudor arch. She was wearing a white trouser suit in a shiny fabric and all eyes turned toward her, and a breath of astonishment was exhaled through the bar, and one of the girls—well, she was ponytailed but from the look of her upper arms was nearing fifty—giggled aloud. The plump man who sat beside Geoffrey said to him, "Specialized tastes, I presume."

Geoffrey felt sorry for the uneasy-looking giantess, and moved over to sit beside her and bought her a drink; thus, he felt, saving her face. He could not keep his bad eye hidden from her forever.

"That looks nasty," she said, peering at it. "Have you rubbed it with gold?"

"No," he said, surprised. "Should I?"

"Yes," she said, "you don't exactly rub, you roll. You roll the evil away."

And she demonstrated, taking off her wedding ring and rolling it over the infected eye. The metal was surprisingly smooth and silky, and afterward the eye felt soothed.

"Yes, but see here," he said, "I'm not evil. I know it looks evil, but that's the eye, not me. I'm a nice guy, really."

"There's something you don't want to see, I expect," she said. Her own eyes were luminous and perfect. They had a pinkish glitter which he assumed was a reflection from the little red satin lampshades. He looked at the other girls, who had a shadowy quality, as if very little stood between them and nothingness, and then at Ruth; it was as if she were rough-hewn in granite, and the sculptor had left suddenly to go to lunch and never came back, but he was grateful for her substance.

"Frankly," he said, "nothing ever seems quite real to me. None of it's what I meant, and I'm fifty-one today. Too late to start again."

She said nothing, but handed him the ring.

"You'd better keep that," she said.

"But it's your wedding ring."

She shrugged. He felt around his eye. Already the swelling was subsiding and the itching less acute.

"Is that the gold?" he asked.

"Of course."

He knew it wasn't and was elated, freed and grateful. It seemed to him that something amazing had happened: that he was cured of a disease he never knew he had—that is, of loss of faith.

He bought a bottle of champagne from the bartender and took it and her up to his room. A customer or so sniggered as they went, but he didn't care.

"It's not looks that count," he said.

"It is," she said bleakly. She liked to have the light out, and to be beneath the covers, and he was not averse to this. He and his wife had started their married life this way, until his wife had started reading the higher-quality women's magazines and decided that sex, nudity, and physical imperfection were nothing to be ashamed of. It was, he had felt at the time, an unfairly unilateral decision, but he said nothing. His wife had a good body—he hadn't. His wife had also, under the influence, he felt, of the same magazines, developed a liking for oral sex and odd positions, which embarrassed him. Ruth liked simply to lie beneath him, which was perhaps just as well. She told him that her husband had complained of her unadventurousness, but what could she do?

He stayed at the TraveLodge for a full week, and paid Ruth's bill for that time. On Monday morning his eye was completely healed, nor did the infection return afterward. Ruth was compliant and docile: she seemed dazed. She talked very little about herself, nor did he ask questions.

One night he woke to find her crying.

"What's the matter?" he asked.

"I'm crying for a friend of mine, a neighbor. The only one I ever really got on with. She died three years ago. I don't forget her. She killed herself."

"Why?"

"She had a fight with her husband. Her name was Bubbles and she had two children. He hit her and she took offense. She went home to her mother, leaving him with the children. She wanted to teach him a lesson; everyone said she should, he was always coming home drunk. But the very next day he moved a girlfriend into the house to look after the children and made her pregnant, so when Bubbles wanted to move back home, she couldn't. So she drank a bottle of whiskey and took pills and her mother found her, dead in the bedroom she grew up in."

"Those kinds of things happen. It's no one's fault."

"Anyway," said Ruth, "that's all over now. It's every woman for herself. I shall never cry again. I expect I was crying for myself, really."

He laid his head between her large breasts and heard the slow beat of her heart. He had never, he thought, heard a beat so slow, and commented upon it.

"I have cold blood," she said. "It moves slowly. I am cold-blooded, and it's getting colder every day."

It occurred to him that they could stay together; that he could leave his wife, which he thought perhaps was what his wife wanted, and the long, dark, decorous nights could go on forever, but she said she couldn't. There was too much she had to do.

"What do you have to do? What does a woman have to do?"

She laughed and said she was taking up arms against God Himself. Lucifer had tried and failed, but he was male. She thought she might do better, being female.

**17** On Monday morning Ruth rose healed from her bed in the TraveLodge, said good-bye forever to her clear-eyed lover, and went to the outskirts of the city, where she stopped at the door of a large detached house with many windows, some of them barred, set in the middle of damp greenery. Shrubs had been planted in an orderly fashion and were of the kind bred to need minimum care.

Ruth rang the bell marked "Visitors." Mrs. Trumper opened the door. Mrs. Trumper was in her early sixties and had many broken veins in her cheeks. She had a large-jawed face, unkind eyes, and her middle ran to fat and slack. To many of her residents she appeared large indeed, but to Ruth she appeared quite small.

"Well?" asked Mrs. Trumper, in not a very friendly fashion, but not too unfriendly, to be on the safe side: one of her old ladies had died the previous week and the room thus vacated was still not filled. This large person might have a suitable parent to offer, possibly even one of the best kind—an old woman suffering from premature senility, but not yet incontinent. Government grants were often quite substantial for such cases, an incontinence allowance being automatically payable once senility was diagnosed, whether or not it was appropriate.

"Mrs. Trumper?" asked Ruth.

"Yes." Mrs. Trumper stubbed out her cigarette, just in case the visitor was from the local health authority. Not only did the caller have a large, dominant jaw but it was Mrs. Trumper's experience that women who allowed hairs to grow from face moles had a self-righteous nature. Such people were often employed finding fault with others.

"I hear you have a vacancy for a live-in domestic," said Ruth, and Mrs. Trumper examined her cigarette and found that, with care, it could just about be reignited. She took Ruth into her office. She always had such vacancies. There are far more helpless old people in the world than there are young ones prepared to look after them.

Ruth described herself as being from the north, recently widowed, and with experience in the care of the elderly.

Mrs. Trumper did not inquire closely into these claims. The applicant was strong, which was necessary, and clean, which kept the visitors happy. It did not matter whether or not she was honest, since the residents had very little property to steal, being of an age when, surely, possessions meant little, and, more to the point, lived in rooms that would clutter up in no time if they were allowed to do as they liked.

Mrs. Trumper took Ruth through the house, explaining her duties and the nature of Restwood, for this was the name of the establishment. In the front of the house, with the privilege of a room to themselves and a view over the garden, lived the relatives of the rich. There was one titled lady who had to be especially well looked after, for she gave the place class; she had her own bathroom. In the back of the house, sharing in twos, threes, or fours, were the relatives of the less affluent. The home charged triple the basic pension allowance per week, which kept it more or less exclusive.

"The old are all the same," said Mrs. Trumper, "so exclusive's just in the head! Allow no nonsense; take a firm line: remember, they're no different from children. Are you used to children?"

"Yes," said Ruth.

"Then you'll feel at home here," said Mrs. Trumper. "Report any damp or smelly beds at once. And remember, they're cunning: I've known them to smuggle out whole wet mattresses in an attempt to deceive. Of course, I always find out in the end."

"Find out what?" asked Ruth.

"Incontinence!" said Mrs. Trumper.

When residents started wetting the bed, Restwood was not the place for them to be, said Mrs. Trumper.

"They must love it very much here," said Ruth, "to go to such lengths to stay."

"Oh, they do," said Mrs. Trumper. "They do. Sometimes, of course, I overlook it longer than I should. I'm too soft-hearted for my own good."

Ruth's bedroom was small and the bed too short, and her pay was $85 a week. Mrs. Pearl Fisher, Mary Fisher's mother, shared one of the back rooms with Ruby Ivan and Esther Sweet.

"What lovely names you all have," said Ruth the next day, bringing their early morning tea, startling them out of drugged slumber. The visiting doctor prescribed Valium and Mogadon for depression and sleeping disorders, in large quantity. What else could he do? In his opinion, the less the old ladies saw of Restwood the better, and they had nowhere else to go.

Mrs. Fisher, Mrs. Ivan, and Mrs. Sweet seemed quite pleased and surprised at this comment, and thereafter regarded Ruth as a friend. The Restwood staff, in their eyes, divided sharply into two—friend and foe. Mrs. Trumper was foe. Mrs. Trumper watched and waited until her residents wet the bed: then she turned them out, back into the merciless hands of relatives, until a proper nursing home with sheet-changing facilities could be found. And such places, everyone knew, did not exist. There was a bottleneck, here at the very end of the road that was their lives.

Ruth chatted and patted and heaved and combed and wiped and sloshed disinfectant about the place for a week or so, and presently remarked to Mrs. Fisher that she knew her daughter, Mary, but Mrs. Fisher looked at her vacantly and did not respond. Ruth replaced her Valium with vitamin B tablets and her Mogadon with vitamin C and made the same remark a week later.

"Funny you should say that," said Mrs. Fisher. "I don't think anyone ever knows Mary, least of all her own mother, which is me. How is she?"

"She's very well," said Ruth. "She has a new lover."

"Disgusting," said Mrs. Fisher. "She's no better than a little she-cat in heat. Always was. I could see through her from the very start. She belongs to the gutter, and I say that advisedly, because so do I."

She spat. She swung her head, gathering spittle as she went, and spat. She could spit right from the end of the bed to the far corner, over the tops of Mrs. Ivan and Mrs. Sweet, who were gentle souls. They looked depressed. Ruth wiped up the lump of spittle. Its texture was thin and runny, like the white of an old, warm egg.

"She did me a bad turn," observed Mrs. Fisher. "She stole my man. He had money, too. I was half his age, but she was a quarter, so she finished him off twice as soon. Dirty old man. Serves him right. A socialist, too."

Ruth encouraged Mrs. Fisher out of bed and into her metal-frame walker. By the end of a month Mrs. Fisher could walk without a frame, and by the end of six weeks could manage the stairs on her own.

"On your own head be it," said Mrs. Trumper. "It looks good for the visitors, I'll say that; one of our bedriddens leaping up like that. On the other hand, they're less trouble in bed than out of it, you must agree."

Ruth gave Mrs. Fisher beans and apples and coleslaw and brown rice and the grinding pains in her stomach subsided. She hiccuped and farted a great deal, and Mrs. Ivan and Mrs. Sweet became restive.

"You need a room to yourself," said Ruth. "You're not bedridden, you have a right to personal space."

She had explained the concept of the latter to Mrs. Fisher. That individuals had rights was something Mrs. Fisher had never before understood. She had assumed that people just got what they could, in a basically hostile world. She took to the new doctrine with alacrity.

"I have a right to two strips of bacon," said Mrs. Fisher, up and down the corridors. "A person has a right not to be hungry." Or, "I'll have two baths a week if I want; I have a right." Or, "After all I've done for my country, I have a right to a rubber ring that keeps my arse comfortable all night through." Or, "A mother has a right to spit/fart/blow her nose with her fingers when and as she wants." And grunts and groans of assent would echo in and out of the bedrooms and even into the common room, where the ambulants sat around the wall in plastic armchairs and stared at television programs they did not, could not, and would not understand.

Visitors, instead of being acquiescent and grateful, started asking for extra pillows, saucers with cups, and for the water in vases to be changed more often, especially in the dahlia season. "Why don't they look after their own folk, if they're so fussy," asked Mrs. Trumper into her gin, "instead of leaving me to do it?"

Mrs. Trumper was fairly sure the trouble had started with Ruth, and was torn between the desire to fire her and the anxiety as to how she could replace someone so strong, clean, and willing. She was also frightened of Ruth; Ruth was too big. She could snap Mrs. Trumper between forefinger and thumb. Her eyes glittered.

Mrs. Fisher demanded a room of her own. "And where will you get the money to pay for it?" asked Mrs. Trumper. "Your daughter gives us little enough as it is. Out of sight, out of mind, so far as old ladies are concerned, Mrs. Fisher. I've seen it often enough! Of course, people get the end in life they deserve. At the beginning it's all luck: at the end it's all justice. You, Mrs. Sweet, and Mrs. Ivan deserve each other. That's why you're all in the same room."

She liked to have her little jokes with the patients. They rarely understood her, in any case. Sometimes Mrs. Trumper felt very alone.

"I'll write to my daughter myself," said Mrs. Fisher.

"You can't," said Mrs. Trumper, "because you don't have her address."

"Yes, I have," said Mrs. Fisher, "so sucks to you!" She used a far cruder expression in fact, having been, as she kept saying to Ruth, in the gutter.

Mrs. Fisher wrote to her daughter. Ruth dictated the letter.

My dear Mary, it is a long time since you have been to see me. I know you are very busy, but you should sometimes think of the one who reared you and saw you through your difficult years. My lot in life would be much improved if you could pay Mrs. Trumper for me to have a room to myself with my own television. Then I would not miss visitors so much.
With all good wishes to you and yours, and my love to the little ones,

Your loving mother,<br>Pearl

"But she doesn't have little ones," said Mrs. Fisher.

"She does now," said Ruth.

"Fancy that," said Mrs. Fisher. "The cunning bitch! A mother is always the last to know!"

But she didn't seem to want to know more.

Ruth posted Mrs. Fisher's letter herself because so much of the mail somehow never got through. A letter—picked up by Ruth from the mat where it fell—presently came back on scented paper, in Mary Fisher's tiny, delightful hand, saying that more funds were not available, but she hoped her mother was well and happy. She was very busy these days: inflation meant she had to work twice as hard for half as much, and she had many mouths to feed. In fact, if her mother could cut down on the sherry she'd be grateful. She longed for a life as peaceful and tranquil as her mother's, and loved her very much.

"Your poor daughter," said Ruth, "seems to be working so hard! Perhaps you can help her, Mrs. Fisher. Had you ever thought of that? Perhaps a mother should be at her daughter's side, if she possibly can. If it's in her strength to get there."

But Mrs. Fisher just settled back into her new soft cushions, turned on the television, and looked at Ruth in a sideways kind of way, and said sometimes she wondered what Ruth was up to, but she was on her side, whatever it was. Only she wasn't going to go and live with her daughter.

She talked of a certain Nurse Hopkins, who'd been good to her, but who'd come into a fortune and left Restwood. After she'd gone Mrs. Fisher had felt safer just staying in bed.

"That Nurse Hopkins," said Mrs. Fisher, "was short as a teaspoon but wide as a door, and strong with it. Of course you're big as a house. That helps, around here."

"What became of her?"

Nurse Hopkins had gone to work in a hospital for the criminally insane, said Mrs. Fisher, where she'd look no different from anyone else. Ruth would have got on well with her. Everyone could do with a friend. In the meantime she was *not* going to live with her daughter. Why should she do the little bitch a favor?

"But you have to forgive. You could stay with her, just for a short time, surely? You could take a train and go and see her."

"I'm too old."

"You're only seventy-four. It's nothing."

"I suppose I could go," conceded Mrs. Fisher. "One Sunday afternoon, say."

"I'll put you on the train," said Ruth. "I'll buy your return ticket, and telephone through and ask the manservant to meet you."

"Manservant!" said Mrs. Fisher. "I bet there's hanky-panky there!"

"I bet there is, too," said Ruth.

"She can't hide anything from me," said Mrs. Fisher. "I'm into everything! I'll sort her out."

One Sunday morning Ruth removed the placebo tablets from Mrs. Fisher's medicine bottle and replaced them with Valium and Mogadon. On Sunday lunchtime, when Mrs. Fisher was in the dining room, Ruth emptied the copious contents of Ruby's commode into Mrs. Fisher's bed, and brought in a vase of stale dahlias to mask any possible smell, at least for the time being. On Sunday afternoon Ruth put Mrs. Fisher, dressed in her purple and green and dirty black best, on the train to the station nearest the High Tower. She went back to Restwood and rang Garcia from Mrs. Trumper's office and said she was calling from Restwood to let them know that Miss Fisher's mother was coming down for the day and would Garcia meet the train. She was blunt and to the point and put down the receiver before Garcia could consult Mary Fisher.

Ruth sat by the telephone and waited for it to ring, which it presently did. Mary Fisher was on the line. She did not wait to learn whom she might or might not be addressing, but spoke at once in a rather more high-pitched voice than usual.

"This is inexcusable, Mrs. Trumper," asid Mary Fisher. "In the first place, there is simply not a train back this evening. In the second, I should have had at least a week's warning, and in the third, what do you think you are doing, allowing a senile woman to wander about the country in this way, taking trains at will? Anything could happen to her."

"This is not Mrs. Trumper," said Ruth in an assumed voice, one of impeccable gentility, "but a senior member of the staff. Mrs. Trumper is at a funeral. If there is not a train this evening, then the best thing for you to do is to keep your mother overnight and return her in the morning. We could not give you warning because your mother gave us none. She is a human being with full human rights, not a parcel, and can come and go as she wishes. Nor is she senile. She is wonderfully improved in health, lately, for which we are all heartily thankful, and you as her daughter surely must be so, too."

Mary Fisher put down the telephone without attempting any reply, recognizing that on the other end of the line she had an equal opponent. Ruth waited. Presently Garcia rang, saying that Mrs. Fisher would be back on the morning train the following day and requiring someone from Restwood to meet her at the Central Station.

"Of course. Though of course we'll have to charge taxi fares to Miss Fisher's account."

She waited for the phone call to come that disputed the charging of the taxi fares, but none came.

Mrs. Trumper returned from Mrs. Sweet's funeral at six-thirty. Mrs. Sweet had gone downhill rather rapidly since old Mrs. Fisher had left the back room and joined the ambulants. Apparently Mrs. Sweet required for her sustenance a diet of aggravation, resentment, and resignation. Food alone was not enough. Mrs. Trumper, finding Ruth in her office on her return, observed as much, reproachfully.

"The purpose of life should not be its prolongation," said Ruth, "but the manner of its living."

"That's all very well," said Mrs. Trumper, "but it leaves me with an empty bed and a too-rapid turnover of residents. It doesn't look good."

Ruth told Mrs. Trumper that Mrs. Fisher was to be away all night, at her daughter's request.

"So long as she doesn't ask for a rebate," said Mrs. Trumper, "she can do as she likes. Not that I won't miss the old trout. She's not as boring as the rest. In a place like this you could die of boredom. Well, many do. Look at Mrs. Sweet! But at least she left her mattress in a good state."

"I thought I should tell you," said Ruth, "that Mrs. Fisher's bed has been a little damp lately."

"Damp?" cried Mrs. Trumper. "How damp?"

"Very damp."

"Incontinence!" cried Mrs. Trumper, changing her favorable view of Mrs. Fisher, and moved at once to action, lurching to her feet.

"If what you tell me is true," said Mrs. Trumper, as she plodded up the stairs, "this is a serious development. It is my duty to investigate. No one shall say that Restwood is either careless or callous!"

Mrs. Trumper felt and smelled Mrs. Fisher's mattress.

"This is long-term leakage," Mrs. Trumper said, "I can always tell. How long has this been going on?"

"About a month," said Ruth. "I didn't like to tell you. Poor Mrs. Fisher. She can't help it, after all."

"You're fired!" cried Mrs. Trumper, incensed and impetuous. "Look at the state of this mattress!"

It was indeed sodden. Ruth had lately been bringing lager in to Mrs. Fisher, in some quantity, instead of sherry.

Mrs. Trumper rang Mary Fisher and said that on no account was Mrs. Fisher to be returned to Restwood, either the following day or ever. Restwood was a residential hotel for the elderly, not a nursing home for the incontinent.

"I understand there will be higher charges for sheetage and so forth," said Mary Fisher, "and I suppose I have no option but to pay them. But I regard it as blackmail."

"You don't seem to understand," said Mrs. Trumper. "This is cards on the table time; chickens coming home to roost. Your mother is home to roost, Miss Fisher. I will not take her."

"Then what am I to do with her?" wailed Mary Fisher.

"What I've done with her for the last ten years," said Mrs. Trumper. "Look after her and put up with her."

"But I'm not a nurse."

"She doesn't need nursing. She needs TLC."

"What is that? A new drug?" For the first time an element of hope could be heard in Mary Fisher's voice.

"Tender loving care," said Mrs. Trumper, letting the laugh show in her voice.

After a short silence Mary Fisher, who was paying for the call, said, "But Bobbo and I were going on holiday."

"Take her with you. She loves new places, new people."

"Don't be absurd," said Mary Fisher.

"Then stay home," said Mrs. Trumper. "Do you know how long it is since I had a holiday?" And she settled down one-handed to listen to what she called the relative's recitative. With the other hand she cunningly opened, and then poured from, a bottle of gin. Mary Fisher presently gave up the attempt to persuade Mrs. Trumper to keep her mother, and asked for the name of a nursing home where incontinents were welcome.

"There is none," said Mrs. Trumper, in triumph. "There are one or two that will take them in, at a substantial extra charge, but they have waiting lists of from five to ten years."

Mary Fisher openly wept. Mrs. Trumper, satisfied, concluded the conversation. She went up to Ruth's room to say that she was reinstated, but found Ruth already packing.

**18** Mary Fisher lives in the High Tower and considers the nature of love. She does not think it's so easy now. The stars wheel and the tides surge and the salt spray beats upon the thick plate glass, but Mary Fisher's eyes are turned inward; she no longer delights in these things. She could live in Nightbird Drive, or anywhere, for all she notices the glory of nature.

Mary Fisher lives in the High Tower with two children and an angry mother and a distracted lover and a sulky manservant. She feels they devour her living flesh. These days champagne gives Mary Fisher acid indigestion because she can no longer savor each sip, but has to gulp it down before meeting the next domestic emergency.

Smoked salmon is too salty for Bobbo, whose blood pressure is slightly raised, and although Mary Fisher explains that smoked salmon is not in fact a food with high salt levels he will not believe her, and does not like to see her eating what he does not. Tuna sandwiches are frequently served, here as anywhere.

Mary Fisher looks at love and sees that it is complicated. For one thing, she is held in sexual thrall by Bobbo, as indeed quite often the heroine's best friend is held by the hero at the beginning of one of Mary Fisher's books, before a purer, more spiritual love strikes the hero and heroine, and the best friend gets ditched or run over, like Anna Karenina, or obliged to munch arsenic, like Madame Bovary. Such is the fate of best friends.

But Mary Fisher is not the best friend; she is the heroine of her own life, or wants to be. The more she has of Bobbo's body, the more she wants it. She desires his good opinion: she will do anything to have it, even look after his children, her mother, grow old before her time. His good opinion means a good night in bed. Sexual thralldom is as tragic a condition in life as it is in literature. Mary Fisher knows it, but what can she do?

**19** Bobbo couldn't marry Mary Fisher, because the law refused to divorce him from a wife he couldn't produce, who indeed might very well be dead. But nor was the law prepared to declare her dead and himself a widower. Ruth had disappeared—traumatized, Bobbo claimed, by his departure and the accidental burning of her home. Bobbo no longer liked to hear Mary Fisher speak harshly of Ruth. Sometimes he even lamented the fate that led him to Mary Fisher, and true love. He did not deny their love nor wish it undone; just sometimes he could see it would be convenient if it had never happened.

And the High Tower itself was not the place it was. The children pressed dirty palms against snowy surfaces and kicked footballs against shiny glass and sprawled over the backs of sofas, breaking them, and stretched quilts to make trampolines, and tripped and sent family heirlooms flying. Andy, trying to play polo from the back of a Doberman, sent Mary Fisher's great-uncle's grandfather clock crashing to the ground. Mary Fisher wept.

"It was all I had left of the past!"

"Only possessions," said Bobbo.

"The past my foot!" shrieked smelly old Mrs. Fisher. She was back on Mogadon and Valium, prescribed by the doctor, and was now indeed incontinent. "I remember the day your first husband brought it home from a junk shop, and so do you. Your husband who was mine by rights."

And the staff tittered as Mary Fisher sat tearfully beside the fallen clock, its lovely bits and pieces all churned up inside, twanging and jangling faintly, still lively in death.

And still Bobbo would not have the children confined, or restrained, or discriminated against, as he saw it. He thought they had suffered enough. He did not feel responsible for their suffering, but sometimes seemed to feel that Mary Fisher was. He had become a very concerned father, now that they had no mother.

"This is their home now," he said, "and they must feel it. And you are their stepmother, in the eyes of God if not the law."

And Mary Fisher was too confused by the feel of his lips nuzzling her ear to say, "But this is not what I meant. Not what I meant at all!"

Nicola managed to break the Bang & Olufsen hi-fi simply by leaning against it. Mary Fisher had learned not to weep but couldn't help groaning.

"Buy another!" said Bobbo. "You can afford to, after all."

But could she? Keeping the High Tower standing and a sensible edifice, now that its original purpose—the keeping of· sailors away from rocks—was gone, was an expensive business. And agents have to be kept, and servants, typists, accountants— Mary Fisher was obliged to keep not only herself but a whole host of others, rocking gently on the sea of her dubious and possibly even temporary success. As Mary Fisher kept saying, "I am only as good as my last novel." And Bobbo knew that her novels were not "good" at all, but merely salable, a distinction she was afraid to make, for what is salable today is unsalable tomorrow.

And she had expensive tastes. Bobbo did like at least to be able to buy the wine but Mary Fisher's palate was so sensitive it could get through $100 a night with no difficulty, and if there were guests more like ten times that amount.

Not that there were many guests, these days. Those whom Bobbo liked, Mary Fisher didn't, and vice versa. Sometimes it was better just not to have anyone at all. And besides, there were the children, and Nicola had suddenly sprouted heavy breasts for which she was surely far too young. "She takes after her mother," said Bobbo. There was no getting away from it: she did. Nicola and Andy squabbled and shrieked. Such guests as there were left thankfully.

Bobbo stared out of the plate-glass windows of the High Tower onto the foaming sea, and contemplated life and death, and justice and mystery, and someone had to be practical, so it was Mary Fisher. That, she began to understand, is what love does to woman. The material world surges in; tides of practical detail overwhelm the shifting sands of love. The bed creaks at night.

Andy's feet were astonishingly smelly. The Dobermans were forever picking up the scent and tearing through the High Tower barking. And Harness the spaniel was of course now a noticeable member of the High Tower household—Bobbo had retrieved him from the neighbors after the fire, and found him not only traumatized but suffering mites as well, a skin infestation with which he then infected the Dobermans. Scratch, scratch, scratch! Doberman hair, fortunately, is short, but spaniel hair is long, and was everywhere. Nevertheless, Dobermans are powerful dogs, and their scratching shook the floors by day and night; even the stone walls, designed to withstand as powerful seas as nature ever intended, sometimes seemed to tremble in the dark hours of the night; scratch, shake, shudder, shake!

Mercy the cat, also brought to join the household, was vexed and troubled by the change, and became old Mrs. Fisher's familiar; naturally enough, according to Bobbo. Now she was given to leaping on Mary Fisher's lap and secretly sucking away at the silky folds of her dress, as at a nipple. Some form of bleach in the cat's saliva, indeed, left nipple patterns in the fabric which dry cleaning could not remove. In this way Mercy had ruined some of Mary Fisher's loveliest dresses.

"The cat's upset," was all Bobbo would say. "She'll get over it in time. Give her more milk!"

"How long is 'in time'?"

"Years," Bobbo said.

Bobbo went to his office in the city for two days every week. He did not like to let Mary Fisher out of his sight for longer than that. He did not trust Garcia. The rest of the week he worked at home and rather rashly delegated responsibility to his staff. His clientele, thanks to his association with Mary Fisher, now included many writers of great wealth, if not distinction.

Bobbo on the whole was happy. He had more or less what he wanted. He had the family he had always wanted, the home he wanted, the style he wanted. A rich, beautiful, and famous mistress to love and worship him. If she failed in his estimation, he would withdraw his sexual favors for a time, and speak in flattering terms of other pretty, younger women he had encountered, and so brought her, confused and anxious, to heel. These days she was not looking her best, and knew it. Sometimes her fingernails broke and she couldn't be bothered filing, painting, and protecting them, but put the worrying finger in her mouth and tugged with her teeth and pulled the whole top segment of nail off, down to the quick.

Mary Fisher could no longer cry out in the act of love, because old Mrs. Fisher was listening and so were the children. Nicola listened out for Bobbo; Andy for Mary Fisher: he sorted his way through her silken underwear whenever he could. Nicola tried to dress in the way that Mary Fisher did, and looked extraordinary. Mary Fisher suggested to Bobbo that doors and walls should be put where no doors or walls used to be, in order to achieve a degree of privacy, but Bobbo wouldn't hear of it.

"This place is magnificent," said Bobbo. "It would be a shame to turn it into something ordinary. You must be careful, Mary, not to turn into a suburban housewife!"

But that of course was what part of him yearned for her to be, and worked for her to be. To stop work, to cease earning, to wash up: to be what his mother never was. His.

Mary Fisher finished a novel, *The Far Bridge of Desire*, and submitted it to her publishers; it was returned for extensive alterations. She was alarmed, upset, and disconcerted. For if Mary Fisher had lost her touch, if a million million women stirred in their Valium dreams, reached for a Mary Fisher novel, and sank back into slumber again, disappointed, that was tragedy indeed. The loss was not just Mary Fisher's, but theirs. If in Tashkent, in Moose Jaw, in Darwin, and in St. Louis they said, "We needed Mary Fisher and she betrayed us," her misfortune was multiplied a million times.

And why had it happened? She couldn't understand it. She had taken more care with this novel than with many another. She thought that in the end that might make it better. She'd shown it to Bobbo during its writing, as any loving woman would her man, and he had even helped her with it. He'd wanted her heroes to be a little graver, a little less tall . . .

"Like you, you mean, Bobbo?" She'd laughed, but he'd frowned and asked her to be serious—a little more sensitive to the arts and a little less given to blood sport. He'd corrected her grammar, improved her construction, sharpened her plotting, and reproached her for her way of stringing adjective upon adjective, as if words were building blocks and the aim to construct the highest possible tower. Bobbo had gone to college: she, Mary Fisher, had not. He should know. She charmed, but he *knew*.

"But the way I do it *works*," she protested. "Millions of readers can't be wrong. Can they?"

"Darling Mary, indeed they can. It is not the number of readers that count, surely, but the quality of the reader. You are worth more than this. It upsets me to see you selling your talent the way you do, writing trash. You could be a serious writer."

"But I *am* a serious writer."

Trash! She suffered. He enfolded her little limbs in his muscled arms and kissed her better. He did, he did! Sometimes it was all so like her novels. So why wouldn't he believe her, why couldn't he believe what she wrote? Or rather what she used to write, when love was in the head and not in the flesh?

Love was real, and life was everlasting, and endings were happy. Were they not themselves the living proof that romance was real? Bobbo and Mary, happy forever in the High Tower? But Mary Fisher's voice faltered just a little as she proclaimed it.

Mary Fisher rewrote her novel in the old sloppy way, in secret, and regained her publishers' confidence and her own, at least for the meantime.

"Darling," said Bobbo, not sleeping with her for three days—three whole days!—after publication day, "it's not that I'm disappointed in you, it's just that instead of changing the book you should have changed your publishers! Since you can aspire to something higher than a mass market, why don't you?"

"Because it doesn't pay so well," said Mary Fisher harshly, staring at the electricity bill. Until she'd met Jonah, the rich and elderly socialist, she'd been poor. Her father had left home in her infant days and her mother had entertained a gentleman or two to pay the rent, one of whom had been Jonah. Poor Jonah hadn't lasted long, after marrying Mary Fisher. And then a daughter turned up to contest the will. After that Mary Fisher had to fend for herself.

"We have each other," said Bobbo. "Isn't that enough? My practice is building beautifully. If I had your full support behind me it would do even better. Then you wouldn't have to write at all." Bobbo parts her lips with his tongue and her thighs with his body and says he is all hers, and she is all his, and perhaps it is true.

Mary Fisher considered the nature of lust, and the self, and sacrifice. Mary Fisher was not what she had been, and knew it. The little tough nut at the core of her frail being was chipped and breaking. She could feel it. Lust corrodes as love does not. Lust is all hard hammer blows, cracking and splitting. Love is a slippery, velvety cloak to hide in. Lust is real and love is the stuff of dreams, and dreams are what we are made of. A million million women couldn't be wrong. Could they?

Bobbo's blue eyes stared into hers; if she closed her eyes he opened them with his fingers, gently. He wanted her to see the truth.

Part of the truth of life, Mary Fisher now observed, was the sorry nature of its end. Old Mrs. Fisher's body and mind were out of step. The mind stayed bold and wayward and unloving: the body querulously dependent. If she was to be kept quiet she must be tranquilized; if she was tranquilized she drooled and wet the bed, or worse, the brick crevices of the High Tower. The staff complained.

"So what am I to do?" Mary Fisher asked the doctor.

"It's one thing or the other," he said. "There is no perfect solution. She is your mother and you must love her and care for her, as she loved you when you were helpless. That's all you can do."

It's hard to love a mother who has never loved you. Nevertheless, Mary Fisher, presented with her duty, did not avoid it. She tried.

Mary Fisher started and finished a new novel in the space of three months. She called it *Ace of Angels* but her publishers felt it lacked conviction. It was too intricate; it lacked the driving simplicity of her earlier work. A kind of gritty reality kept breaking in. The readers wouldn't like it. One page romance, the next fable, the next social realism! Her publishers looked at each other. Well, she was growing old. How old? No one knew.

It didn't matter to Bobbo how old Mary Fisher was. Bobbo thought she was probably about forty: at any rate she was timeless and her throat was firm and her little hands were white, and the memory of the giantess and the humiliation of his marriage to a freak was fast receding, and he loved Mary Fisher and loved to show it, and he was the maypole around which the tangled skeins of her happiness wound and unwound, strong and firm and forever.

"I heard you! Disgusting! Animals!" cried Mrs. Fisher, popping up from somewhere. "My daughter's fifty if she's a day. I have proof. Want to see her birth certificate?"

"I'm so bored in this crummy place," moaned Nicola, who had put on another ten pounds.

"I'm sick," hiccuped Andy, and was, over everything.

Garcia wasn't there to clean it up—he was at the vet with Harness, whose leg had been badly bitten by one of the Dobermans (not the bitch) whom Harness had tried to mount. Mercy the cat chose that day to urinate in Mrs. Fisher's bed. At least that's what Mrs. Fisher said. The two maids handed in their notice. Garcia was not there to charm them into submission with promissory glances from his liquid brown eyes. Mary Fisher was seen to wash dishes by a photographer from *Vogue*, who called on a speculative appointment, and whom she didn't have the strength to send away.

Bobbo was beginning to find the drive between the city and the High Tower oppressive. Quite often, these days, he stayed overnight at his office, or with friends. Friends?

"Oh, Mary!" said Bobbo. "How can you be jealous? You know I love you. You are the beginning and end of my life!" Except on Wednesday nights, thought Mary Fisher. Then where are you?

One Wednesday night, Mary Fisher wept in the desolation of family love and Garcia heard and stood beside her bed, icily wistful, recalling former times. She asked him to leave but he didn't, and what could she do? He knew too much and too little and if he handed in his notice she would be lost. She knew it: she would be altogether crushed between the mills of the present and the future, with no cushion from the past to insert between them. So she didn't scream as he slipped into her bed. In any case, who would have come? The Dobermans? Mary Fisher wanted to have everything and lose nothing. She always did.

Mary Fisher's *Ace of Angels* was published, but only just.

Garcia asked for a raise. She had no option but to give him one, although Bobbo objected.

"We must be a little careful, surely, Mary?"

"Oh, money!" she pooh-poohed, but she didn't feel it. The last royalty return was way down. Perhaps she was going out of fashion? No one had filmed one of her romances for six years, now she came to think of it.

"How is she looking?" Ruth asked Garcia one day; she telephoned him from time to time, just to see how things in the High Tower were getting on. He would tell her, with alacrity, and without remorse. Mary Fisher no longer inspired his loyalty.

"She is beginning to look old," he said.

**20** Mary Fisher lives in the High Tower and nearly, nearly prefers death to life. Beneath her balcony the great seas beat themselves upon eternal rock. What shall she do to be saved?

Mary Fisher must renounce love, but cannot. And since she cannot, Mary Fisher must be like everyone else. She must take her destined place between the past and the future, limping between the old generation and the new: she cannot escape. She nearly did: almost, she became her own creation.

But I stopped her. I, the she-devil, the creation of her lover, my husband. And she needn't think I'll stop there. I've only just begun.

**21** There is always a living to be earned doing the work that others prefer not to do. Employment can generally be found looking after other people's children, caring for the insane, or guarding imprisoned criminals, cleaning public rest rooms, laying out the dead, or making beds in cheap hotels. Payment is usually small, but enough to keep the recipient alive and strong enough to get to work the next day. There is always, as governments are fond of saying, work for those who want it.

Ruth, after leaving Mrs. Trumper's employ, went straight to a student café in the university area of the city and spent an hour or so drinking coffee and watching the young people who came in and out. She finally approached a pale but handsome young man who sat by himself, with his books, in a corner, and who was treated by the others with interest and respect. They would come up to him, chat for a little, and occasionally money would pass hands, or slips of paper, or small packets.

"I wonder if you could help me," she said.

"That is my profession," he said. "But I usually help the young."

"I am starting my life again," she said, "and I find you can do so much without a diploma, but not everything."

"There are always loopholes," he said. "I see the world, increasingly, as a knot of worms in a bucket, slithering about, looking for loopholes."

"A worm is small and thin," she said, "and I am not."

He agreed that this was so, and someone such as she might well need certificates. They were of course more difficult to organize, being labor-intensive, and skilled labor at that, than either sex or drugs, and would be expensive. But he would see what he could do.

Ruth obtained two certificates of general education, one in English and one in mathematics, for which she paid $50 each. She had him make them out in the name of Vesta Rose, a name that in her childhood she had always longed to have.

Ruth then took a bus to the office where the unemployed went, for the most part vainly, to look for jobs, and said she wanted work as a prison officer. She gave her name as Vesta Rose and produced a false address. She said she had had experience abroad in the caring professions. She produced her certificates. "What a pretty name!" said the girl behind the desk, idly, before looking up at Ruth and wincing. Ruth had scraped her hair tightly back from her face, which made her jaw look longer than usual and her eyes deeper set than ever. She had regained at Restwood the weight she had lost at the TraveLodge. Restwood ladies and staff ate white soft food, high in carbohydrates, low in protein.

"There's no work in the prisons," said the girl.

"I understand there is, at Lucas Hill Hospital."

"Lucas Hill!" said the girl. "That's different! They always have vacancies there. Do you really want to go to Lucas Hill?"

"I have a friend who works there."

"Then you understand the kind of place it is? Our responsibility is toward the employee as well as the employer. It used to be called a PCI, a Prison for the Criminally Insane. They've changed the name but not the inmates. Ha-ha!"

"People like that are to be pitied, not blamed, and certainly not laughed at," said Ruth, and the girl immediately and nervously rang the hospital and made an appointment for Ruth to see the domestic superintendent.

The Lucas Hill Hospital was a pleasant, new building painted in pale green, and with many cheerful murals on the walls, composed by qualified artists in the manner of children. In the corridors patients walked and stood and barked and yelped, and nurses with dispensing trolleys moved amongst them, dosing and injecting.

Doors closed heavily, with electronic clicks; windows were shatterproof. There was no need for keys or bars. Some of the nurses were kind; a few were unkind and enjoyed the exercise of power over the helpless. Some were intelligent, most were not. For the most part, staff worked here whom no one else would employ. They were too fat or too thin or too stupid or too vicious or too black or too white or for one reason or another would simply never ever look good in any front office anywhere.

The domestic superintendent did not inquire too closely into Vesta Rose's past experience. She seemed strong, capable, and clean, and was likely to be less dangerous or disturbed than the inmates, many of whom were murderers or arsonists or given to public acts of gross indecency. Arsonists, here as anywhere, were the most feared: sex offenders the most hated. Some inmates, of course, were there by mistake, or had unwisely pleaded insanity at their trials, and so were now incarcerated for an indefinite time, or until they could prove their sanity, which in Lucas Hill Hospital was a difficult thing to do.

Ruth had some difficulty locating Nurse Hopkins. The staff was two hundred strong: the inmates numbered two thousand. She found her eventually on the Emergency Tranquilizing Team, or ETT, which could be summoned by bleeper within seconds, as necessity on the wards arose. Nurse Hopkins would lay the troublesome, flailing patient out and lean on him or her while a tranquilizing injection was administered.

"I love this job," she said to Ruth, over coffee in the cafeteria. "You get to meet such interesting people, and I like to be useful."

"Women do!" said Ruth.

"Someone has to do the dangerous work," said Nurse Hopkins, showing Ruth the scars she had received from hidden knives and gnashing teeth. "But it's better than standing around watching people die. I used to work in an old people's home. Have you ever done that, Vesta?"

"Never," said Vesta Rose, with a clear conscience.

"Don't," said Nurse Hopkins, with fervor.

The two women got on so well they agreed to share a bedroom together in the nursing block.

"I feel safe with you," said Nurse Hopkins. "A lot of the staff here are nuttier than the patients."

Nurse Hopkins was four feet eleven inches high and weighed two hundred pounds. She had some trouble with her thyroid gland. Her parents, reporting her to the doctor when she was twelve as sluggish, had been required to feed her thyroid extract, fashionable at the time, which had only exacerbated her problem. She felt very cold much of the time, and wore many sweaters, mostly bought from the Goodwill shop.

"Freaks! That's what we two are," Nurse Hopkins would remark, not infrequently.

Nurse Hopkins had several hundred thousand dollars in the bank, left to her by guilty parents, but she enjoyed the security and regularity of working at Lucas Hill Hospital, among people more peculiar than she. Ruth suggested that they push their beds together, end to end, and remove the footboards, so that Ruth's toes could be covered at night, and Nurse Hopkins not to be drafty. One so long, and one so short!

"Mixed together," said Nurse Hopkins, "we'd make two proper people, though still a bit on the heavy side."

Ruth applied for work in the dental department of the hospital. It was a busy place. There was an epidemic of biting; many patients were so incorrigible in this respect that their teeth had to be removed altogether. Other patients had teeth too rotten to be saved. The dentist was an elderly man who came from New Zealand, where many a proud father's present to his daughter on her eighteenth birthday was to pay for the extraction of her teeth and the provision of even, handsome, painless, false ones. He prided himself on his extraction rate, and was grateful to Ruth for her strong, firm, swift hands. Only in a domestic situation, it appeared, was she clumsy, as if her hands had learned to protest long before her mind.

"No broken teeth and bleeding jaws now you're around," he'd say. He drank a great deal. The dentistry he specialized in—the art of extraction—had quite gone out of fashion, and the only work he could obtain now was in government service.

"Still, it's something to be useful!" he liked to say. "These poor people—the dregs of humanity. But they have their rights to healthy jaws the same as anyone else."

He admired the strength and size of Ruth's teeth.

"But I would have preferred to be born with little white pearly ones," she said.

"Then have them," he said. "Whip your old ones out, and fit brand-new."

"I mean to," she said. "But first things first. And I have lots of time."

"Women don't have lots of time," the dentist observed. "Unlike men."

"I mean to put the clock back," she said.

"No one can do that."

"Anyone can do anything," she replied, "if they have the will and they have the money."

"We are as God made us," he protested.

"That isn't true," she said. "We are here in this world to improve upon his original idea. To create justice, truth, and beauty where He so obviously and lamentably failed."

When work in the dental department slackened, Ruth would help out in the occupational therapy department. Here half the classes made raffia baskets, which the other half would then unravel. Union regulations forbade the selling of goods made by prison labor, and the argument, frequently offered, that this was a hospital, not a prison, cut no ice. Every home where there was a sickbed, or even a case of measles, would qualify for exemption, once Lucas Hill Hospital was allowed indulgence. Besides, who out there in the outside world wants raffia baskets? Better unwind, unravel. Occupation is all: possessions meaningless.

On Saturday afternoons visitors were allowed in, and on Saturday evenings the prison officers would hold a party with the fruit, cake, and wine the visitors had left behind. The inmates could not, for the most part, and in the opinion of the officers, appreciate these delicacies, and experience showed that if given them they became restive and given to complaint. Some even cried, which was an act of regression, and put the day of their release yet further into the future.

To cry in Lucas Hill was a sign of both ingratitude and madness, and was frowned upon. Lucas Hill was a particularly pleasant place the feeling was, staffed by people trained and anxious to help, and to be sane was to be grateful for being there.

Sometimes inmates would escape; they would be promptly brought back by the police and locked into the quiet cell, to teach them gratitude. This special cell was padded and contained nothing except a lidless lavatory bowl. There was a grille in the door, through which cheese sandwiches and cans of Coke could be pushed, and a glass panel that the staff could see through but the inmates not. Patients often stayed in the cell for a week before the door was opened. When it was, they were indeed grateful for what they had and seldom ran away again.

In Ruth's spare time she went to secretarial and bookkeeping classes in the city. These were offered almost free by the government to women and girls. The work was not popular with men, who prefer to dictate letters and spend money rather than account for it. Ruth was a hardworking pupil and progressed rapidly in her studies.

"Why do you do it?" Nurse Hopkins asked.

"Because I am ambitious," said Ruth.

"But you're not planting to leave Lucas Hill?" Nurse Hopkins was worried, but not, Ruth thought, worried enough.

"Not without you," said Ruth, and Nurse Hopkins shivered with pleasure, and Ruth was gratified.

One Tuesday evening, when Ruth felt that she had sufficiently mastered the basics of accounting and bookkeeping, she took the bus into the city. She got off at Park Avenue, where Bobbo's office was, on the tenth floor of a new office block, marble-halled, and with its vestibules alive with the sound of splashing fountain water. Opposite this building was a fast-food restaurant, and here Ruth sat, taking care to be in a dark corner, eating baked potatoes, sour cream, and chopped chives at her leisure. She watched and waited for Bobbo to emerge. She had not seen her husband since the day she took her children to the High Tower.

Bobbo came out with a young blond girl, clearly not Mary Fisher but of the same type, and presumably some kind of secretary or assistant, since she looked both adoring and diffident. He kissed the young woman very lightly and casually good-bye, and they parted their ways, but for a little while she stood looking after him, with longing and love. He did not look back. Bobbo seemed confident, prosperous, and well able to inspire love. He hailed a taxi and, running back across the road to catch it, seemed for a moment to look straight in at Ruth. But he failed to recognize her. Ruth thought that after all that was not strange: they now inhabited different worlds. Hers was unknown to him: those on the right side of everything take care to know as little as possible about those on the wrong side. The poor, exploited, and oppressed, however, love to know about their masters, to gaze at their faces in the paper, to marvel at their love affairs, to discover their foibles. It is, after all, the only return they can extract from the daily brutal using-up of their lives. So Ruth would recognize Bobbo, lover and accountant; Bobbo would not recognize Ruth, hospital ward orderly and abandoned mother. Convenient, indeed essential, as it was to her plans not be recognized, still she resented it. Any lingering spark of compunction, any trace of those qualities traditionally associated with women—such as sweetness, the capacity to forgive, forbearance, and gentleness—were at that moment quite obliterated.

Bobbo caught his taxi. Ruth waited until all the lights on the tenth floor were extinguished, and then made her way to Bobbo's office. She let herself in with the master key she had taken care to pocket before setting fire to No. 19 Nightbird Drive. Her plans, vague then, centered mostly on the notion that she must practice doing what she was not allowed to do, were now fully formulated.

Bobbo's office had lately been redecorated in tone of buff and cream. Ruth thought that was Mary Fisher's taste. Bobbo's own room seemed more like a hotel lounge than an office; it contained a sofa long and soft enough for agreeable dalliance, with, presumably, such members of Bobbo's staff as took his fancy. That would not be to Mary Fisher's taste. The staff themselves —some six of them—shared, with many filing cabinets—rather more cramped quarters than Bobbo himself enjoyed. But that was the way of the world.

Ruth drew the blinds and lit a single spotlight and with the aid of this and one of Bobbo's pens began work on the files marked "Clients' Account" and listed under "A." She moved theoretical sums from one ledger to another, signed a check for $10,000 payable to Bobbo and made out on his business account into his personal account, typed an envelope to his bank, enclosed a formal "with compliments" slip, and added it to the pile of letters awaiting postage. It was the custom of Bobbo's office to mail letters in the morning, not the evening, since they were then less subject to loss and delay. She made herself a cup of office coffee, tried the sofa for comfort, tidied up after herself, adjusted the photograph of Mary Fisher, went through the personal drawers of the staff and discovered a love letter or so, kept in the office no doubt to be safe from husbandly eyes, left, locked up properly, and went back to Lucas Hill and the room she shared with Nurse Hopkins.

This process she repeated every week, peacefully working through the files from "A" to "Z," until a great many dollars indeed had been transferred into Bobbo's personal account from his clients' accounts. She removed any reference to these transactions on Bobbo's bank statements by simply removing zeros with Liquid Paper. It had always been Bobbo's custom to file his bank statements unread, apart from a glance and a groan at his current account. Those who deal professionally with the affairs of others seldom pay proper attention to their own. Nevertheless, Ruth wanted to be on the safe side, although it seemed unlikely that he had changed in this, any more than in his amatory habits: the love of a woman, given and received, will do so much, no more. Bobbo loved Mary Fisher, but liked giving and receiving pleasure from passing strangers, as many people, female as well as male, do.

It was from the same motive, the need to be on the safe side, that Ruth presently suggested to Nurse Hopkins that it would be more comfortable if they slept side by side rather than toe to toe. Ruth could put up with uncovered feet, since summer was coming, and would keep Nurse Hopkins warm enough by simple body heat. Nurse Hopkins agreed. The beds were moved, and there was much cuddling, kissing, and sexual experimentation between the two women.

"Women like us," said Nurse Hopkins, singing around the hospital, "must learn to stick together. People think because you're not the same shape as other people you're not interested in sex, but it isn't so."

Sexual activity seemed to have a tonic effect on Nurse Hopkins: her menstrual cycle became regular, her eyes brightened, she lost weight, divested herself of many layers of sweaters, and moved briskly about the hospital.

When Ruth had worked through Bobbo's files, and put "Z" firmly and gladly back on its shelf, she had the following conversation with Nurse Hopkins:

"My dear, don't you ever get bored here? The same screams and yells day after day; the same manic strugglings; the same injections; the same frog-marches to the quiet cell. Nothing ever happens! For the patients it may be eventful, too eventful even: for us it is not."

"I know what you mean," said Nurse Hopkins.

"Out there in the world," said Ruth, "everything is possible and exciting. We can be different women: we can tap our own energies and the energies of women like us—women shut away in homes performing sometimes menial tasks, sometimes graceful women trapped by love and duty into lives they never meant, and driven by necessity into jobs they loathe and which slowly kill them. We can get out there into the exciting world of business, of money and profit and loss, and help them, too . . ."

"I thought all that was supposed to be very boring," said Nurse Hopkins.

"That is just a tale put about by men to keep the women out of it," said Ruth. "And there waiting, too, is that other world of power—of judges and priests and doctors, the ones who tell the women what to do and how to think—that's a wonderful world as well. When ideas and power go hand in hand—I can't tell you how exciting they find it!"

"I daresay," said Nurse Hopkins, "but how do the likes of us get into it?"

Ruth whispered into Nurse Hopkins's ear.

"But that would take money," said Nurse Hopkins.

"Exactly," said Ruth.

The farewell party for the two nurses was gratifying; tears and laughter flowed free, and wine was rather rashly offered to the patients. A general overexcitement throughout the hospital kept the ETT busy, and Nurse Hopkins's replacement, a Haitian lady, knelt on a patient so hard that she broke a rib; but the other members of the team thought that no bad thing. If their arrival was feared, rather than looked forward to, they might have to work less hard.

Ruth and Nurse Hopkins found empty office premises down at the far end of Park Avenue, where those at the top end seldom go, for here the tall new gracious towers give way to shabby buildings, and the street narrows and is lined not by the awnings of smart restaurants, but by garbage bags piled high against dirty shop fronts. The telephone exchange is the same, however, at both ends of the avenue, so callers cannot tell whether they are speaking to the rich end or the sleazy end. Here, with Nurse Hopkins's money, Ruth started the Vesta Rose Employment Agency.

The agency specialized in finding secretarial work for women coming back into the labor market—either from choice or through necessity—women who had good skills but lacked worldly confidence after years of domesticity. Those who signed on with the Vesta Rose Agency would receive retraining in secretarial skills and what Ruth called "assertiveness training." The agency also organized day-care facilities for the babies and young children of those on its books, and shopping and delivery service for their convenience, so that workers did not have to shop during their lunch hours, but were able to rest, as male workers are expected to do, and even go home on the bus unencumbered by shopping bags. For these privileges they paid dearly, but were pleased to do so.

Nurse Hopkins ran the day-care center on the top floor of the agency building, and if from time to time she used tranquilizers on the more obstreperous children, she was at least trained and qualified to do so, and knew what side effects to look out for. She and Ruth shared an apartment a block away from the agency.

"Wherever you go," said Nurse Hopkins, "I will follow. I have never been so happy in my life."

Within a month or so of its opening, the Vesta Rose Agency was functioning efficiently and was even in profit. The women on its books—and they emerged out of the suburbs on bus and train by the hundreds—were grateful, patient, responsible, and hardworking; and for the most part, after a little training by Ruth, regarded office work as simplicity itself; as should anyone who has dealt daily with the intricacies of sibling rivalry and the subtleties of marital accord, or discord. Vesta Roses, as they came to be called, were soon in great demand by employers throughtout the city; the agency even enjoyed a little fame; it was held up as a success story; an example to the weak-willed and complaining of what women could do if they really tried, if they hadn't been fortunate enough to marry well! Vesta Rose herself remained elusive, and although she was prepared to give an occasional telephone interview to the press, she would never appear in person, nor permit herself to be photographed. Nurse Hopkins did all that part of it, and did it very well.

"You see," said Ruth, "how little need there was to hide yourself away from the world."

"But I needed you," said Nurse Hopkins, "before I could do it. People aren't meant to be on their own."

Within six months Ruth had placed typists, secretaries, book-keepers, and catering staff in most spheres of city life. Clients appreciated her guarantee to replace unsatisfactory staff at two hours' notice but seldom had to make use of it, so dutiful and grateful were this new breed of Vesta Roses. The agency took only five percent of their wages, plus additional charges for child care, shopping, and—as time went on—a laundry and dry-cleaning service. There was no suggestion that they should claim their rights as Women with a capital "W," and insist that their menfolk take an equal share in child care and household chores—merely an understanding that this end, though laudable, was for most women too remote to be attainable, and that in the meantime practical help was essential, if the woman was to continue with her traditional role of homemaker and also earn. Their husbands would come home from work, dinner would be set before them, clean shirts laid out for them, the television set tuned in to the program of their choice, and the flow of the household continue as it had always done. That way content-ment lay, if not justice, and the turning of the man to the woman in the peace of the marital bed, and her to him, was perhaps all the compensation required for the evident injustices of married life in the modern world.

Every week, when her staff arrived to take their wages, minus five percent—or sometimes as much as fifty percent if they had made use of all the agency services—Ruth would chat with them, one by one; discuss their troubles, try to solve them: find out a little, or sometimes a lot, if she was interested, about the firms they worked for. Sometimes she would ask for a few dis-creet services which they were happy enough to fulfill, and which could reduce the commission payable quite substantially.

Ruth had to wait eight months before someone rang from Bobbo's office. She used the time to start what banks call a "little healthy movement" in the joint account that she and Bobbo had once enjoyed, until his removal of all but a few cents of the funds therein shortly before the burning of the matrimonial home, and that had lain quiescent since. That is, she paid in, sometimes by check, by mail, and sometimes in cash, and in person, a hundred dollars here, a thousand dollars there, from sums legitimately hers and raised from the Vesta Rose business, and would on occasion withdraw twenty dollars here, fifty there, in cash or by check, using Bobbo's name. Once she withdrew two thousand dollars from Bobbo's personal account, signing in his name, and paid it into the joint account; that required further nocturnal visits to Bobbo's office, and more work with Liquid Paper when his quarterly bank statements came through. However, the junior clerk at the bank was a pleasant young woman, Olga, from the Vesta Rose Agency, who had an autistic child in the day-care center cared for by Nurse Hopkins, and so was anxious enough to be helpful: it was she who moved Bobbo's current account statement card from the monthly section to the quarterly, thus saving Ruth considerable work and anxiety. It was Olga, also, who ensured that the joint account statements were simply lost from the mail and never reached Bobbo.

When Bobbo's office rang the agency it was to require the services of two reliable, well-qualified women—a part-time secretary for Wednesdays, and a girl to help out on Mondays and Fridays—days spent by Bobbo at the High Tower. Could the Vesta Rose Agency, with its reputation for reliability, help?

Of course! Ruth sent Elsie Flower for the Wednesday job. Elsie was little and sweet and, in looks, rather similar to Mary Fisher. She had little hands which flew over the typewriter, and her neck bent prettily over the machine. She bowed her neck as she bowed her mind, as if forever expecting some not altogether unpleasant blow to fall. She was bored with her husband—she had told Ruth so. She was in the mood for adventure. Ruth thought Elsie would do well enough for Bobbo.

For the Monday and Friday job, Ruth sent Marlene Fagin. Marlene had four teenage sons by three different fathers, all disappeared, and so was particularly grateful for the agency's shopping and delivery service. The sheer weight of food for five—and they were particularly fond of Coca-Cola, which is a heavy substance to carry about in quantity—had exhausted her as no office work ever could. She was perfectly prepared to render whatever small bookkeeping adjustments in Bobbo's books Ruth required, especially as sometimes Ruth remarked that delivering to the outer suburbs—where Marlene lived—could never be economically sound.

On the first Friday when Elsie came to collect her wages, Ruth asked, "And how was your employer?"

"Saucy," said Elsie. "And with his lady friend's photograph looking on!"

"How saucy?"

"He put his hand through my hair and said how silky it was."

"Did you mind?"

"Should I have?" Vesta Roses liked to take instruction from Ruth. It paid. Sometimes she would waive commission altogether.

"I always think," said Ruth, "one should meet experience as it comes, and not turn away. Lift's short. The things one regrets, I find, are not the things one did, but the things one didn't do."

"I see," said Elsie, gladly. Sometimes all a woman needs is permission.

Marlene reported the following week that Bobbo's office was bubbling with gossip about Elsie and the boss and that she'd stayed after hours on Wednesday night.

"I know," said Ruth. "She's put in a claim for overtime."

And so Elsie had, and so she did for the ensuing six weeks, and on the seventh, when she came to collect her wages, she said to Ruth, "It's more than just sex. You've no idea how nice he is. How terribly, terribly special!"

"Is it love?"

Elsie bit her lower lip with little pearly teeth and cast down her blue eyes. "I don't know," she said. "But oh, he's such a wonderful lover!"

"What about your husband, Elsie?"

"I love him," said Elsie, "but I'm not in love with him. If you know what I mean."

"Oh, I do!" said Ruth.

"But I don't know what he feels about me," said Elsie.

"Have you told him—what's he called, Bobbo?—what you feel?" asked Ruth.

"Oh, I couldn't," said Elsie. "It's not like that. He's so, somehow, important."

"But so are you," said Ruth. "Tell him you love him or he may think this is the kind of thing you do all the time. He may not know it's important to you."

"But I don't want to frighten him off," said Elsie.

"Now, how could telling him the truth do that?"

The next day Bobbo himself rang through and asked for a replacement for Elsie, under the agency guarantee.

"Certainly, sir," said Ruth, in the voice of Vesta Rose, one of extreme gentility and rather high-pitched. "Might I ask what the trouble is? Her speeds are excellent. She is very well recommended."

"That is as may be," said Bobbo, "but she is overemotional. And under the terms of your guarantee, may I remind you, no questions are asked but a replacement provided."

"Very well, sir," said Ruth.

"Don't I know your voice from somewhere?" he inquired.

"I hardly think so, sir," said Ruth.

"I know what it is," he said. "You remind me of my mother."

"I am glad to hear it, sir," she said. "Now, if you'd be so kind as to ask Mrs. Flower to call in at our office—"

"She's gone already," said Bobbo, "in floods of tears. God knows why. I suppose you don't have any men on your books?"

"No, sir."

"A pity," he said, and rang off.

Elsie came weeping to Ruth. She had told her husband, she said, that she was in love with Bobbo and her husband had said, "That's the last straw" and left. She had told Bobbo what had happened and how much she loved him and he had said, "But this is blackmail!" and told her she was fired, that he had no

127

time for histrionics in the office, there was too much work to do.

"I would have thought," said Elsie, "you could get on in the world by sleeping with your boss. That you'd get a raise, or extra leave, or a promotion or something. But you don't. You just get fired quicker. I've made such a mess of my life."

"Life is all lessons," said Ruth. "The thing to do is to learn by them. I suppose really you'd like to make a new start."

"Oh, yes," said Elsie, who hadn't until that moment.

"Somewhere far away, and peaceful, and full of handsome men, like New Zealand."

"I've always wanted to go to New Zealand," said Elsie. "But how would I ever afford the fare?"

"How indeed?" said Ruth. "How circumscribed our lives are for shortage of something as simple as money!"

"None of it's fair!" said Elsie. "I only told my husband to shake him up a bit; how was I to know it would shake him up too much? That bastard Bobbo! I want to get even."

"You could always write a letter to his lady friend," said Ruth.

"She has a right to know what's going on."

"What a wonderful idea!" cried Elsie Flower, and did so. She received no reply.

"I don't suppose she even cares," complained Elsie.

"I expect she does," said Ruth.

"I'm so unhappy," said Elsie. "He used me and discarded me as if I was worth nothing."

"I feel responsible," said Ruth, "because I sent you there. So the Vesta Rose Agency is giving you these."

And she handed Elsie two air tickets, first class, one to Lucerne via Swissair, and another from Lucerne to Auckland, via Qantas.

"First class!" marveled Elsie. "Women usually don't like me, yet here you are being so wonderful to me!"

"There's just a little task I'd like you to do for me," said Ruth. "In Switzerland."

"Nothing illegal?" Elsie, like anyone, became nervous when everything seemed to be going too well.

"Good heavens, no," said Ruth. "Just a little financial dealing. The tax laws here are iniquitous, as everyone knows, and particularly against women. It's all so much better in Switzerland."

"I'll do whatever I can," said Elsie, easily enough convinced, as indeed people are when only a vague morality stands between them and what they want.

"But look," said Elsie, examining the tickets. "The one to Auckland is made out in the name of Olivia Honey."

"Oh, yes," said Ruth. "I quite forgot. And there's this!" She handed Elsie a passport, easily enough obtained from the young man in the student café. This, too, was made out in the name of Olivia Honey, and contained a very flattering photograph of Elsie: the agency kept such photographs of all its employees. Her age was given as twenty-one.

"It's a lovely name," said Elsie.

"Some would think so," said Ruth. "Some wouldn't."

"I never liked Elsie," said Elsie. "And look, I've lost five years!"

"Ungained them," said Ruth. "Five years of extra life, or extra youth, which, after all, is the same thing."

"I'll do it!" said Elsie.

"I knew you would," said Ruth. "Who wouldn't?"

Ruth transferred two million or so dollars from Bobbo's personal account into his and her joint account. She wrote to a Swiss bank in Lucerne—Swiss banks ask no questions—in Bobbo's name, opening a joint account and depositing a check for the two million dollars. Olga intercepted the confirm-in-person-please note on the manager's desk, and the transaction went through unquestioned. (In return Nurse Hopkins formally adopted Olga's autistic child, thus setting Olga free to resume her career as a singer, which she forthwith and successfully did.) Ruth flew to Lucerne herself and there met Elsie, moved the money into an account that Elsie had just opened, and waited for it to be cleared. Elsie withdrew the money in cash, handed it over to Ruth, kissed her fondly good-bye, and disappeared into the airport as Olivia Honey.

Ruth returned briefly to Nurse Hopkins and the Vesta Rose Agency.

"My dear," she said, "the time has come to say good-bye."

Nurse Hopkins wept.

"You must never feel sorry for yourself," said Ruth, "and you must never blame your parents for your misfortunes. They may have given you thyroid tablets as a child, but they did it out of love and concern for you, and most importantly, they left you money. Money is to be used, not hoarded. I am leaving you the Vesta Rose Agency to run and Olga's little boy to love. These two legacies will keep you busy enough, especially the latter: too busy for you to grieve for me much."

"But what is in that suitcase?" asked Nurse Hopkins, cheering up. "And where are you going?"

"There is money in the suitcase," said Ruth. "And I am going into my future."

She was only just in time. The following week the accountants moved into Bobbo's office to do the annual audit. They stayed a remarkably long time, holding up the work of the place, and Bobbo thought at first that this was a symptom of their inefficiency.

But presently a policeman came to visit him.

"I have no idea what you're talking about," said Bobbo.

"Don't try to bluff it out," said the policeman. "We have a fair idea what happened. So little Miss Elsie Flower let you down. Where were the pair of you going to start again? South America?"

"Elsie Flower?" said Bobbo. "Who's she?" And in all honesty he couldn't remember. Bosses seldom remember typists.

**22** Mary Fisher is distraught. What is happening to her life? Her happiness is held in a broken bucket, and it is all leaking away. First a letter in the mail from a girl who claims to be Bobbo's mistress. Bobbo denies it, of course he does, but Mary Fisher knows by now that such letters are usually true and that this one certainly is. She understands now that unhappiness must follow happiness, misfortune good fortune. That to love is to be vulnerable to fate and to be vulnerable is to invite attack by fate. Bobbo stops denying it, says, very well, it was true but it was over, it meant nothing, you know what typists are, they come today and go tomorrow, ha-ha; dearest Mary, I love only you, you are the light of my life, the lantern of my path; how can you demean yourself to be so downcast by the letter of a nobody? A malicious nobody, at that? And Mary Fisher forgives him; what can she do but forgive him; except lose him, and if she loses him she thinks she will die.

And how can she not forgive him, and how can she not forgive him with the imprint of Garcia's fingers still recorded in her flesh? But oh, what is sauce for the gander is poison for the goose.

Mary Fisher lives in the High Tower at the edge of the sea, surrounded by walls of privacy and privilege, at one with nature. Once she dallied with the world, but now, with love, the world comes surging in. First it was her lover's children, then her mother, now it comes in the shape of a policeman, knocking at the door. How the Dobermans bark and dance!

She knows nothing: Bobbo knows nothing. "This misfortune comes from an unkind fate," she says.

"It comes from your guilt," he says.

Mary Fisher reels as if from a blow. Is everything her fault? Of course. She it was, after all, who inspired the love that ruined them. She it was, in the carefree days of un-love, who commanded Bobbo to take her home, who allowed Ruth to be discarded, who lost his children their real mother—there is no end to her responsibilities.

Bobbo weeps. "It is all so like a bad dream," he says, denying now even that the ground she walks upon is real.

In her mind the High Tower totters, crumbles, stands derelict. It might as well.

Garcia stands at doors and listens. He delights in the downfall of the dwellers in the High Tower. "The higher you build," he says to me, "the farther you fall. It is natural justice," he says.

"Not so natural," I say, and laugh. She-devils are beyond nature: they create themselves out of nothing.

Policemen come to the tower when Mary Fisher is not in; they search it, they find the folded letter from Elsie Flower in her jewel box, in the locked drawer, along with strings of pearls from early lovers and emerald brooches, which she keeps, out of the weakness of nostalgia, secret from her Bobbo. She has never quite forsaken the past for the present: never quite.

Garcia leads them to the jewel box. He has no shame, no qualms. She has betrayed him. Once Mary Fisher was the sun in his heaven; now she is nothing; she mingled herself with Bobbo, and became as he was—nothing.

The police close Bobbo's office, seal his doors, confiscate his books.

"I do not understand," is all he can say. "Mary, I love you."

Mary Fisher sits in the High Tower and waits for friends to gather around, but they don't. What can they say? Your fancy man, your lover, has embezzled our money. We are writers, people of talent, unworldly, trusting, and what have you done to us? Your fancy man, not so fancy, was about to run off with his typist, but she disappeared with the loot! Out of kindness to Mary Fisher, friends stay silent.

Bobbo sits in the High Tower and grows morose. He fails to shave, his chin becomes flabby, the hair on his jowls turns gray. "Do you believe in me, my love?" he asks.

"I believe in you," says Mary Fisher.

"Then save me," he says.

Mary Fisher hires the most expensive lawyers in the world. She flies them in from distant parts. English is not their native tongue: she must hire an interpreter, too. "It will be expensive," they warn her. "This kind of case can go on for years."

"Oh, Bobbo," says Mary Fisher, "if only you had not been unfaithful to me, this would never have happened," and even as she says it, sees love drain out of his eyes: and somehow, as a stream, which seeks its own level, love flows over into hers, and her fate is sealed. The less he loves, the more she will.

There is a knock at the door of the High Tower at three in the morning. It is the police. Mary Fisher telephones her lawyers at their expensive hotel, but they cannot understand what she is saying. Their interpreter is elsewhere. Bobbo is led away.

In the morning the interpreter is found and says, "Incarceration is nine-tenths of the law. We'll do what we can." And so her lawyers do, but it seems to be marvelously little. They apply for bail and settle down to prepare the case, as well as one, a difficult and tricky one, for political asylum for themselves. They appreciate a country full of Mary Fishers!

Mary Fisher puts one house on the market: it is not a good time for selling houses. Her lawyers say one house is not enough. How many do you have? Only three? Oh, dear! Well, that will just about see us through to the trial. This is fixed for some nine months hence. Such delays are inevitable, the times being what they are, and the judge appointed being a certain Henry Bissop, an unpredictable, popular, and busy man. But they will do what they can to release her Bobbo on bail, to return him to Mary Fisher's arms.

Garcia no longer visits Mary Fisher at night. He has altogether lost his appetite for Mary Fisher. He enjoys the sound of her weeping. Why should he try to stop it?

Mary Fisher lies awake and alone at night, and weeps for lack of Bobbo. He is her child, her father, her everyone, her everything. Her only consolation is that in prison he can hardly be unfaithful to her.

Beyond the High Tower the constellations wheel, as if nothing untoward had happened here on earth. Mary Fisher wonders if Bobbo can see the sky from his prison cell, and if he thinks of her. Somehow, when she visits him, the matter does not come up.

**23** Judge Henry Bissop lived in great luxury in a house on a hill overlooking the city. The house was newly built in a kind of reddish puckered cement varnished to a high gloss, in imitation of wet brick. It was set in an acre of plastic grass, which could be cared for by hosing down rather than mowing. The judge feared robbers, having met so many, so the house was studded with locks and bars and shutters, but a virtue had been made out of necessity and all had been forged in intricate wrought iron by master craftsmen. From some angles it looked like a castle, from others a bungalow.

Inside, the purple carpets were of the deepest pile available, the many little lampshades were of the finest pink satin trimmed with gold braid, and the plump sofas were of the most expensive orange leather imaginable. Walls were paneled in glossy mahogany veneer, or lined with crimson flock paper, of the kind found in Indian restaurants. This was Lady Bissop's taste, not the judge's, but he let her have her head in this, as in nothing else. He liked to watch the expression on the faces of visitors as he showed them into the living room, to catch the flicker of dismay, quickly suppressed. It was to the observation of such fleeting facial flickers in court, and his quick interpretation of them, that much of his reputation for wisdom was owed, and he could not get enough of them.

No use, thought the judge, having a natural talent for spotting liars—you had to work at it, develop it, watch the rubbing of ears, the licking of lips, the quick slide of the eyes.

"Like the decor?"

"Why, yes, Judge. Wonderful!"

"All my wife's idea. She has a fine, natural talent, don't you agree?"

"I certainly do, Judge."

"And isn't she a lovely girl!"

"She certainly is. You're a lucky man, Judge."

Lies, all lies!

Lady Bissop, although considerably younger than her husband, was no beauty. He had chosen her on this account. He feared the seduction of beautiful things: he feared life's irony. He had heard and seen too much of it. Go to a concert, and a thief runs off with your harp. Have your wife's portrait painted and she runs off with the artist. Stare too long at the beauty of a flower, marvel at the nature of creation, and your grip on the universe is instantly loosened, and all kinds of random events rush in to overwhelm you. If Judge Bissop had a vision of God it was of a great scriptwriter in the sky, churning out B-feature scripts, studded with coincidence, improbable events, and unbelievable motives.

So Lady Bissop was not the kind of woman whom painters ran off with or for whom Troy fell; she had a large nose and a receding chin and rather dull eyes and a disappointed expression. She had borne the judge two sons, who took after her, and were quiet and well behaved. The judge disciplined them in the same way as he himself had been disciplined as a child—that is, if they did anything to annoy him he would scoop up whatever was nearest—sand, earth, salt—and stuff their mouths with it. It was uncomfortable, but it was safe (up to a point), quick, and effective. The children took care, as they grew up, not to annoy or disrupt. He thought they were the happier for it, and if Lady Bissop did not agree, she did not say so.

The judge himself, even at sixty, was a wonderfully handsome man: tall, broad-shouldered, even-featured, self-controlled. His hair was plentiful, snowy-white, and cut weekly. When the judiciary was having its photograph taken Judge Bissop would be pushed to the fore, for he looked like what a judge should be—distinguished, wise, firm but kindly.

The judge took his work seriously. He knew he must stand above and beyond the common man, guarding himself from error, protecting himself from corruption. He knew how rare a man he was, how very few there were prepared to wield the fine rapier-blade of justice within the vulnerable substance of society: how difficult it was to dispose of another man's life when he personally had done you no particular harm, how peculiar to steal his time away in yearly chunks—twelve months for this, eighteen for that, a dozen years for the other. How disconcerting to be the one to say this is bad, this is worse, for this there's hell to pay! But there it was. And it was, when it came to it, a vocation. He had been born to it.

The judge's family had to play their part; it was the penalty exacted by fate for their closeness to so exceptional a man. They had to be careful not to wake him in the night, not to overtire him with their demands or irritate him with chattering. They had to exist—for a man functions best if he ventures out into the world from a domestic setting in which his restless sexual and procreative energies are given liberty. But they could not be seen (or heard) to exist too much.

Lady Bissop had spent many nights pacing up and down with crying infants in those rooms of the house farthest from the judge's bedroom, and whispering to them, as they grew older, in the early mornings, so that their childish prattle did not wake him. And why should she not? Did not the future of some wretched miscreant depend upon his midmorning humor? Five years incarcerated, or fifteen?

Judge Bissop did not want to think that he was cut off from the ebb and flow of normal life. He needed to keep his ear to the ground, to catch tremors of popular discontent, the rumblings of public opinion. He was, after all, the public's servant; but he must be devious, must look ahead. Deal harshly with a rapist now, and you would forestall the day when the masses demanded the forcible castration of all sex offenders. Deal lightly with a bigamist today, and postpone the tomorrow when all marriage laws were revoked. The people's voice must be heard, but how to hear it, when the people insist on having their judges out of earshot, sitting on thrones, dressed in wigs, in courts more like theaters than rooms of general consultation?

So the judge read the popular papers whenever he found time, and fell into easy conversation, whenever he could, with those few members of the public who crossed his path—newspaper sellers, waiters, his barber, program sellers at the opera house, members of his own domestic staff.

His wife had lately hired, through an employment agency in the city, a very tall, ugly woman who went by the name of Polly Patch. Her references were excellent, and she had two certificates in general education and one in child care (advanced). His wife had taken her on as live-in household help.

The judge did not think she would last long. Lady Bissop hired and fired staff impetuously. One day, being lonely, she would confide her troubles to the maid, the next, feeling better, she would complain that she was being taken advantage of and demand that she leave at once. There was no redress: domestic staff depend upon the whims of those they cosset. The judge hoped that Polly Patch would stay for at least a month or so. He found ugly people interesting. It seemed to him that they were in touch with a reality, a knowledge that he himself had been denied. His path through the world, he felt, had been too easy, made so by his good looks, his background, his intelligence. He was his parents' glory, his school's triumph, his profession's pride, but where was *he*? He thought that Polly Patch, lumbering through a doorway, engaged in the menial business of child care, might well have the secrets of reality at her square fingertips, and be the one to impart them. Then he would know what was really going on. A man, even a judge, has to have something or someone to measure himself against, if he is to know what sort of person he is. If the judge so much as flicked his fingers at his wife and children, they melted into the wallpaper; they disappeared. Hard to make Polly Patch disappear: her surfaces were like sandpaper—the coarse kind, not easily worn smooth.

Miss Patch, to his relief, showed no signs of taking advantage of his wife, and seemed in no danger of being dismissed. If anything, Lady Bissop seemed a little in awe of her. Polly Patch had rather deep-set eyes, which from time to time glittered pinkly—perhaps only because of Lady Bissop's fondness for rosy lighting—but which nevertheless seemed to invoke respect. She was, the judge estimated, twice his wife's size, and had twice her intelligence. Her looks, no doubt, mitigated against her in the labor and marriage markets, which was why she was reduced to nannying. Or perhaps, as did so many women, she simply longed for a home, for sofas and beds and fires and doors locked at night against intruders, and a daily ritual of work and leisure, and the soft purr of the washing machine renewing and restoring, and since she could not achieve this for herself—for it has to be done in the lower reaches of society with a man's money and consent—did the next best thing, and entered someone else's home as servant.

The judge was at first a little suspicious of this new member of his household: the men and women who appeared before him, the criminals, the misfits, the losers, were for the most part unprepossessing (if they were not, they stood a better chance of being acquitted, juries being what they are). He knew it was a mistake to assume that, because all convicted criminals are ugly, all ugly people are criminals, but the uneasy feeling remained that this was true. Perhaps she was the thin end of some robber wedge, come to case the joint, steal all his worldly possessions. One day he might come home and find the purple carpets, the orange sofas, the appalling silver cutlery in modern design, the surrealist paintings, all gone, stolen by a gang for whom she was the cat's-paw. He came to doubt it. She had a natural taste: she turned the coverlets of the children's quilts inside out, making them a browny gold instead of bright tan, so that he did not have to wince when he went into their rooms to kiss them good night. (He did this every night, ritually, knowing quite well they only pretended to be asleep. Why should his family be different from the rest of the world, why any less deceitful?) And although to have a natural taste was not a bar to criminal activities, it did not predispose toward them. It was, on the contrary, more likely to create a victim—the robbed and not the robber. The judge grew to trust her. He liked the way she scooped up the children, tucking them underarm with ease, carrying them quickly out of earshot if they squabbled or whined.

It was over the matter of the peanut butter that Polly Patch finally won his heart. Henry Bissop allowed no peanut butter in his house, irrationally and irascibly, driven to unreason and fury by the unintelligence of those with whom it was his fate to work and live—by, in fact, the rest of the world. It had lately and unwisely been brought to his notice, by a group of social statisticians investigating the causes of crime, that the majority of people who committed them had consumed, in the time around the act, an unusually large amount of peanut butter.

Such spurious statistics incensed him—it was obvious to the judge that the peanut butter involved was consumed in prison while awaiting trial (peanut butter being a staple of prison diet). Those responsible for the study had foolishly reckoned that criminality commenced on the day the prisoner was found guilty, rather than on the day he had actually committed the crime. So when defending counsel put forward this and other convenient but ill-considered statistics in an attempt to show their clients in a favorable light, or so that blame would pass from them onto society itself—barristers have the habit of blaming unemployment, or pollution of the mind by lead poisoning, or poor nutrition, or lack of education for their clients' malfeasance—the judge had only to stare at the barrister hard and say, "I never have peanut butter in my house. I don't want my children growing up criminal," and their voices would falter and their cases crumble in confusion. It was his joke, but they didn't find it funny.

The judge lived in a glimmering hope that one day his wife Maureen would resist the domestic peanut butter ruling, for peanut butter was the children's favorite food, and dispute the offered statistic, and take him to task, but she never did, any more than his barristers. Perhaps it was too much to expect that she should show intelligence where highly trained lawyers could not. Nevertheless, he writhed and moaned in the face of their incomprehension and inflicted upon them, as punishment, a peanut-butterless house.

Lady Bissop, with the years, had become even more pliable, more acquiescent, less argumentative. He felt she was turning back into a child, that she grew down as others grew up. It was his fear that one day soon he would find himself stuffing salt into her mouth as if she were his daughter, not his wife. It was in the attempt to keep his wife a properly functioning adult female, and not someone fast regressing into a pubescent girl-child, that he subjected her to extreme sexual practices; or so he later explained himself to Polly Patch. As long as he nipped her nipples with his teeth so that she cried out, her breasts would not disappear. As long as he could tug and twist her pubic hair, it would continue to grow. It was for her own good.

Another of the penalties of judgehood, or so he explained it to Polly, was the sadistic energies it stimulated in the judiciary. That same shivering pang of pain and pleasure mixed, which the description of a violent death or a nasty accident sends darting through the loins of the hearer, darts and lingers in the loins of those who are entitled, indeed required, to inflict pain, to pass sentence. Normally, because the judiciary is so very old and enfeebled, the pang, which contains in it the necessity of sexual release, passes all but unnoticed. But Judge Bissop was vigorous and sexually active, and Lady Bissop, as a wife, was at the mercy of the demands of her husband's profession. As a doctor's wife has to answer the phone, as a sailor's wife has to put up with his absences, so a judge's wife has to put up with his cruelty.

The judge, in her interests as well as his own, would save up a month's sentencing and do it all in a week, at the end of which Lady Bissop would be too bruised and bleeding to come down to breakfast but would at least have the next three weeks to recover. He was not unreasonable. She had wanted the status and money that went with being a judge's wife, and must now take the rough with the smooth.

The judge confided all this and more to Polly Patch. He had come to trust her after the way she had dealt with the matter of the peanut butter. They'd sat in the purple lounge by the gas flicker-fire after the children were in bed and Lady Bissop gone to soak in a long hot bath.

"You may have wondered why I allow no peanut butter in this house!" the judge had said, eventually. "The reason is because most people convicted of violent crimes have recently eaten so much of it."

Polly Patch thought for a while. "Perhaps," she said, "it's because most people who appear in court charged with violent crimes have been in custody for some weeks, months, even years —so overcrowded are our prisons these days—and peanut butter is no doubt a staple of prison diet, being cheap and rich in protein. Peanut butter is neither here nor there, when considering the crime, or the character of the criminal. Your children can eat it safely!"

The judge had grasped her large hand warmly; he felt it was safe to trust her with his confidences. She paid attention to the content of what was said, not the status of the speaker. That was rare. He valued her. If he had not already married Maureen, he thought he might well have chosen Polly Patch. How pleasant it would be, he thought, to have someone close who was not in awe of him. They were the same height, too, which he liked. He had a tendency, he knew, to bully those smaller than he, and so many were, particularly women. The judge was able to discuss his cases with her, and found the burden of his sentencing much lighter, and much less sexually stimulating, and his treatment of Lady Bissop therefore less extreme, which relieved the judge of anxiety but made him melancholy—a more passive and pleasant version of the emotions of unease, driving a man not to action but to contemplation.

"Swings and roundabouts," he'd say, sadly. "The sum of human misery is always the same—it is the judge's job to shift it a little, where it most fairly lies. But gain fairness here and you lose it there! My wife just happens to be the one who loses. Fairness is a seesaw, and I am at its fulcrum. Impartiality sits at one end, Lady Bissop at the other, and doesn't she keep coming down with a bump!"

He talked about a wife who'd murdered her husband by slow poison over a period of three years. But then the husband had been slowly murdering the wife by his cruelty over a longer period—some six or seven years. She'd started to use the poison the day her cancer was diagnosed. The cancer went into remission the day he died. What did Polly Patch think?

Polly Patch's eyes glittered and she said death came to everyone in the end. It was the manner of living that was important.

"If she'd change her plea to insanity, at least I could just send her to a secure mental hospital," the judge said, but Polly Patch did not think this a good idea. They discussed whether the murderess should receive seven years imprisonment, five years, or three. Odd numbers seem preferable to even, when it comes to murder. Premeditation weighed against her, provocation for her. The law must be seen to exact some punishment, or the country would be littered with dead husbands; but not too severe a punishment, or dead wives would become more of a problem than they were already.

They settled for three years, with some clear hints of sympathy in the judge's remarks, so she was more likely to receive an early probation.

"Sentencing is like marking essays," said Polly Patch. "B minus, C plus plus, D plus minus, and so forth."

"Quite so," said the judge, "but it's much more exciting."

Early in her employment Polly Patch asked for time off to go to the dentist, and every time she went she came back with a tooth either totally missing or ground down to the bone.

"I hope you are going to a good dentist," said Lady Bissop to Polly, tentatively enough. She wondered why it was necessary for Polly's large and evidently strong teeth to have to go, but did not like to ask outright for fear of offending her. She did not want Polly to hand in her notice. On the contrary, she wanted her to stay forever; for the judge was fond of her, and in the shadow of her protection the children grew lively and looked happy; and the house ran smoothly, and the judge, less nervous about his sentencing after his talks with Polly, left her, Lady Bissop, alone at night, and had all but forgotten his uxorious passion for bondage and whips, for which—once she had recovered from the initial humiliation of having her servant preferred to herself as far as conversation was concerned—she could only be grateful.

"The best dentist in the city," said Polly, a little thickly. "And certainly the most expensive."

"What exactly are you having done?" asked Lady Bissop cautiously.

"I am having my jaw remodeled," said Polly, "with an eye to my future," and Lady Bissop thought, Poor thing, what's the use? If you took back the jawline it would make the brow look more like Frankenstein's than ever.

"I suppose you are right to try and improve on nature," she said, still doubtful.

"It is not a question of right," said Polly firmly. "But it is what I mean to do. It's just annoying that it all takes so long. Never mind. I am employing the time usefully."

"God places us in the world for a purpose," said Lady Bissop. "We should surely put up with what He gives us, in the way of nose, teeth, and so forth."

"His ways are far too mysterious," said Polly, "for me to put up with them anymore."

Lady Bissop had been brought up to believe that a woman's function was to adjust herself to the times she lived in and the household she dwelt in, and that God worked His purposes out through the consent of the humble and faithful, and there was to be no arguing about these things. She crossed herself, alarmed. All the same she did not want to lose Polly.

"So long as it doesn't frighten the children," she said, "I suppose I can't object."

The children seemed happy enough with Polly's gaping jaw. They would peer down into the black hole of her mouth and shriek with delight: dragons lived down there, they declared. Dragons and demons. They drew pictures of demons and dragons and Polly pinned them to the walls. Lady Bissop worried in case the children got nightmares. They never did. The whole household slept peacefully through the night: judge, wife, nanny, children, and all.

The children went to bed at eight; Lady Bissop followed after at ten. The judge and Polly stayed together before the fire until midnight, and whatever happened, happened.

Justice Bissop had a particularly interesting case on his hands which he would discuss at length with Polly. The case had been hanging fire for months while the defendant's lawyers tried to organize their defense, and failed. The defendant's common-law wife kept interfering, dismissing counsel and hiring others.

"Loyalty in women is an amazing thing," said the judge. "The worse the man, the blinder the woman. I have often noticed it."

The case concerned an accountant who had been cheating his clients in a minor way for years—failing to pay over interest received on monies he'd held on their behalf and holding on to this money unduly long. It was a practice common enough with accountants. The temptation was great, especially in periods of high interest rates, but of course technically illegal. Later, however, the scoundrel had done worse: he had invested monies held in trust for clients in quick, sure-fire in-and-out currency speculation, for which fortunately he had a knack: an uncanny way of knowing the direction in which currency rates would move. His clients, of course, did not get the profits; they vanished out of his books and presumably into his pocket.

The accountant professed his total innocence of these early malfeasances and claimed someone had been tampering with his books. "White-collar criminals," observed the judge, "are always stubborn in the denial of their guilt. They feel secure in their ability to pull the wool over the world's eyes. Blue-collar workers, on the contrary, are all too eager to confess, sometimes to a great deal more than they need—and then fling themselves upon the court's mercy."

The accountant's house had burned down, and many of his files and records with it, thus confusing the issue.

"How convenient!" remarked Polly, and she and the judge had laughed knowingly.

"This man's audacity knows no bounds," said the judge. "His early frauds having escaped detection, he proceeded to large-scale embezzlement. Over a period of a few months he transferred large sums—amounting to millions of dollars—into his own account, and from there into the Swiss bank account of a young woman with whom he had been having an affair."

"His mistress!" said Polly. "And I suppose then he meant just to change his name and start a new life with her?"

"That is certainly the inference."

"What about his poor wife?" asked Polly. "I suppose he was married. Such people usually are."

"She disappeared some time back, after the fire."

"How convenient," said Polly. "I think he's lucky to be up merely for fraud, and not for arson and murder as well!"

"A man of considerable sexual energy," said the judge, stretching his long, underused limbs and looking at her heavy, downy legs. She wore white socks and white fluffy slippers which contrasted strongly and sharply with her dark skin and general unfluffiness and made him contemplate the line between reality and illusion, fact and artifice, and held his mind in a curious suspension, whose only relief, he began to see, would be violent physical contact with her, some kind of sexual mauling.

"Once he'd got rid of his wife he went to live with his mistress, a writer of trashy novels. I must ask my wife if she's read any. But all the time he was planning the great flight, the new life, with someone altogether different, and on his clients' money, too."

"It doesn't look good for him," said Polly Patch.

"It certainly doesn't," said the judge. Her breasts were larger than life. Well, so was she.

"So what went wrong?"

"Something did. Probably his Swiss Miss took off with the money; or perhaps he was waiting for a call from her: we don't know. The accountants moved in, got suspicious, the police were called, and that was that."

"Never trust a woman," observed Polly Patch, and the judge was glad she was unfashionable enough to indulge in the kind of sexist remarks that had once kept conversations so lively, and animation flashing between the sexes.

"Of course that's the prosecution's case," said Polly.

"I suppose so," said the judge. "But the defense is going to have a hard time knocking holes in it."

"I hope he doesn't get away with it," said Polly. "He sounds a very distasteful and dangerous kind of man."

The judge stared into the dark cave entrance of her mouth. She spoke thickly. His wife had assured him that as soon as the gums had healed Polly would have false teeth fitted, at least as a temporary measure, while waiting for the cosmetic surgery that would take three inches out of her jaw. He longed to talk about it.

"Does it hurt?" he asked at last.

"Of course it hurts," she said. "It's meant to hurt. Anything that's worth achieving has its price. And, by corollary, if you are prepared to pay that price you can achieve almost anything. In this particular case I am paying with physical pain. Hans Andersen's little mermaid wanted legs instead of a tail, so that she could be properly loved by her Prince. She was given legs, and by inference the gap where they join at the top, and after that every step she took was like stepping on knives. Well, what did she expect? That was the penalty. And, like her, I welcome it. I don't complain."

"Did he love her," asked the judge, "in return?"

"Temporarily," said Polly Patch. The firelight glinted on her black hair, making it reddish. The judge took her hand in his. It looked as if it should be warm, but it was cold. She brought the conversation back to the accountant.

"Those who are most trusted," said Polly Patch, "sin most if they betray that trust."

"But their temptations are greater," said the judge. "Justice must always be tinged with mercy, and with understanding."

"How much mercy did he show his clients?" asked Polly, her fingers moving with surprising delicacy inside his enclosing hand. "And they were writers, artists, people ill fitted to look after themselves in a cruel world."

The judge, who so often saw writers before him in the role of plagiarists, libelers, and breachers of the Copyright Act, was not so sure that they deserved much pity.

"How long will you give him?" she asked. They sat closer together now, his skinny gray-flanneled thigh running alongside her firm broad one. At any minute now Lady Bissop would be back from her bath.

"A year," he said, "or so."

"A year or so! But you gave that poor mad dying woman three whole years! And he deserves so much more. A man in a position of trust, who coldly and callously and with intent cheats and defrauds and spits his insolence at a society that has done nothing but help him. There will be uproar! You will never be Lord Chief Justice if you are so lenient."

"Ah, but," he said, "a single year to a middle-class man, accustomed to good living and high social station, is equal to five for anyone else. One bears in mind the humiliation he suffers, the destruction of his family, the loss of friends, career, pension, everything."

"Ordinary people," she said, "for the most part are impetuous: they err by accident; the middle classes err by design. The penalties should be doubled, not halved."

He put his other hand over her mouth to stop her talking, which meant that he had to leave his chair and crouch above her. Once the mouth was covered he felt less endangered, less likely to be engulfed.

She shook herself free of him and stood with her back toward the fire, silhouetted against the leaping flames. There was a sudden increase in the flames and crackles behind her.

"You must listen to what I say," she said, "because I am the voice of the people, or as near to it as you will ever get."

"I hear you," he said. And indeed she stood blotting out the light, as the Statue of Liberty does in New York Harbor, or the figure of justice on the law courts in London: the law itself, taken solid form. He took notice of her, and of what she had to say, which was perhaps the same thing.

Lady Bissop came in, in the navy toweling dressing gown he most disliked.

"Maureen," said the judge, "do go to bed!"

Lady Bissop asked tentatively if she could see the judge alone. Polly Patch obligingly left the room.

"Please don't do anything unwise," said Lady Bissop. "Polly might leave, and then what would I do? I've come to depend upon her so."

"My dear," said the judge, "please leave me to be the best judge of what's best for you."

And Lady Bissop, reassured, went to bed and the judge took himself off with Polly to the spare room, where he stayed for two hours. He was a conscientious man and would spend only so much of the night in revelry—he needed to be fresh for the morning. Polly understood, as she understood so much, and did not press him to stay.

The next morning Polly was at the breakfast table as usual, performing her duties, wiping chins, finding shoelaces, positive and cheerful, and Lady Bissop had had a good night's sleep, free of her husband's conjugal attentions, and her various bruises and abrasions given a chance to heal, and she was well able to see the advantages of the new arrangement. She even went into the city to have her hair done, so suddenly lifted were her spirits, and her morale.

The judge, finding a more willing sexual partner in Polly than in his wife, was relieved of guilt, and looking around his world could see little wrong with it. He was almost happy. He permitted his children more latitude. They were allowed to play in the garden, now that his nervousness in case they damaged a plant by kicking a ball had abated. He watched his wife sink back into childishness and even that did not distress him. He now decided to spread his sentencing sessions more evenly over the month, and although this caused some confusion to his staff they quickly adjusted to the new regime. The judge spent pleasurable if hardworking hours with Polly by night, binding her hand and foot to the bed, beating her with an old-fashioned bamboo carpet beater.

"Am I hurting you?" he'd ask.

"Of course you are," she'd reply politely.

"I'm not a sadist," he once said. "This is merely the effect of the work I do."

"I understand," she said, "perfectly. What you are expected to do is unnatural and this is your response."

He almost loved her. He thought she was immeasurably wise.

Lady Bissop decided that perhaps purple was too strong a color for the carpets and settled on a tawny-red shade, in eighty percent natural wool, and for a time the household seemed much like any other, if you left out what happened nightly in the spare room. Lady Bissop even began to entertain a little, as her husband's suspicions of her friends grew less acute, and he felt less convinced they were either laughing at him or making mental notes of the layout of the house, the better to burgle it.

The question of bail for the accountant came up. Polly Patch opposed it.

"But he's been waiting in prison for a full year," said the judge. "And without trial!"

"But we all know he's guilty," said Polly. "And of far worse things than embezzlement. Save your pity for those who deserve it. Good family men, blue-collar workers, those who act on impulse, those who're not likely to go back on their word—they're the ones who deserve bail. But is this man going to honor his bond?"

"The money's being put up by his mistress. The woman must be spending a fortune on him. If he can call out this response in her, he can't be all bad."

"On the contrary," said Polly. "She loved him and he betrayed her. He will do it again. He lived with her but slept with other women. He was preparing to abandon her. Why should he be true to her now? No! Save the poor woman her money. No bail, say I! He will merely abscond."

The judge turned down the request. Bobbo went back to prison to await trial.

The dentist fitted Polly Patch with a row of shiny temporary teeth, so that she now talked less thickly and more precisely. The judge was rather sorry. He had liked the thunderous rumble of ill-defined sound that for a time came out of the dark labyrinth of her throat. He had enjoyed thrusting his tongue into the raw chasm where once her teeth had been, rasping it over the little filed points to which her molars had been reduced. She did, however, look a little more ordinary now; she fitted in better with the rest of the household.

Sometimes he wondered where Polly Patch came from and where she was going; but not often. He was used to people appearing before him out of nothing, into the vivid central color of the court, before disappearing again into the grayness of its perimeter, and perhaps because of his profession rather than in spite of it he asked few questions. He did not have an inquiring mind. He did not need one. A judge waits for facts to present themselves: he does not have to nuzzle them out. Others do that for him.

Polly Patch told him one night that sexual energy illuminated the universe: it must be shone like a torch into its darkest corners. Only then would there be no shame, no guilt, no war. She said that pain and pleasure were one, and that to do what one willed was the whole of the law.

Spoken, as these words were, in harsh tones, from a gaping mouth (for her teeth had gone back to the dentist for reshaping), they had the power of oracle. He thought on reflection that it was the oracle of Hades, not Olympus; of hell, not heaven. Up there on Olympus, where he'd been raised, where the mountain of reason pierces the sky of the intellect, the talk was all of how the soul suffered if the senses were gratified. Polly Patch would not allow it. She claimed, as the Devil would, that the senses and the soul were one: that gratifying one was to gratify the other.

Polly Patch went on a diet of eight hundred calories a day, but lost no weight. No one could understand it. Lady Bissop, on the same diet, lost fifteen pounds in a month, and became so emaciated that the judge felt a renewal of his sexual interest in her—the more unfortunate she seemed, alas, the more he appreciated her—but she shrieked so loudly he felt obliged to return to the spare room once more and the more stoical and better-padded Polly.

The accountant's case came up for its preliminary hearing. Much anger was felt because the accused was uncooperative, and would not pass on information to the police as to the whereabouts of his lady accomplice, thus preventing the recovery of the stolen money. She had worked in his office for a time, been fired—presumably to pull the wool over the eyes of the staff—left her husband, flown to Lucerne—and there the trail had been lost.

"How did he look in the dock?" asked Polly Patch.

"Unexceptional," said Judge Bissop. "He had the gray skin of a man who's been in prison a long time, and the muddy complexion that goes with prison food."

"I daresay he's used to caviar and smoked salmon," said Polly. "Poor thing!"

"Save your pity," said the judge. "He is ruthless and without remorse. He clings to his story. He's stubborn."

"How long will you give him?"

"The case hasn't even come to trial," protested the judge. "We don't know what the jury will say. But I'd reckon five years."

"Not enough," said Polly Patch.

"Not enough for what?" He was teasing her. He held the carpet beater over her buttocks. When he brought it down and raised it again she would have a neat pattern of weals on her flesh.

"Not enough for my purposes," she said.

"Seven years!" he exclaimed.

"That will do!" she said, and he brought the beater down so hard that for once she seemed to feel it, and shrieked so loud the sound could be heard through the house and the little boys stirred in their slumber, and Lady Bissop sighed a sleeping moan, dreaming as she was of lacing canned mushroom soup with pepper, and an owl outside hooted into the blackness.

"The sound of a devil leaving hell," he exclaimed, sucking the essence from the bruised flesh, and whether he was talking about him or her who was to say? He began to see that perhaps he belonged to Hades, where the soul and body are one, and not to Olympus after all. Criminals must take their chance and so must judges. The pain of one was the pleasure of the other. Nightly he rammed the message home, bruising the distinction, blurring the divisions between the holy and the unholy, the white and the black, marking and pulping flesh to make it spirit.

"Of course," he said to Polly Patch one night, in relation to the accountant, who now seemed to obsess him, "they might tempt him to plead insanity. Then he could have an indeterminate sentence, in some secure mental institution, and never get out. Perhaps that's the best thing to do with a man who's not just an embezzler but in all probability an arsonist and a murderer as well."

"I think it a weakness in the judiciary," said Polly Patch, "to allow insanity as a plea. Judges must face human evil head-on, and not sidestep into concepts of mental ill health. It is the crime that must be judged, and not the motive for that crime, or the reason. The function of the judge is to punish, not to cure, reform, or forgive."

It was a long time since Judge Bissop had heard such opinions so firmly put. He took her words as symptomatic of changing public opinion. The needle of government had been swung for many years firmly over to the left, and the public had been vociferous in its demand for stiffer penalties for crimes against the person rather than against property. But now the needle was shaking, and quivering, and preparing for violent movement; a sharp swing to the right, and property and money would again be sacrosanct and human pain and inconvenience but a passing thing. He welcomed it.

When finally the accountant came to trial it seemed reasonable to Judge Bissop that he should receive a severe sentence. The man's two children were in court for some of the trial, chewing gum and in general apathetic, and seeming not to care one way or another what happened to their parent. They were dressed sloppily, and reminded him of someone, but he couldn't remember whom. He thought they should have been presented for the occasion better combed and washed and dressed, and that their demeanor and attire amounted to insolence to the court.

In view of the seriousness of the charges—cold, calculated, and deliberate fraud by someone in a position of trust—he could not, as he pointed out to the defense in his summing-up, consider any notion of a suspended sentence, even bearing in mind the many months the accused had spent in custody. Delays in the hearing had been of the accused's own making, since he refused to admit moral responsibility for his crimes, made no attempt at restitution, even declined to give the police the information they required regarding his coconspirator. Let the defense not believe he was a lenient judge—he was a fair one. The accused had callously abandoned a wife and taken two or more mistresses, thereby causing distress to many, and although a citizen's private life was his own affair and no business of the court's—which the jury should remember in reaching their verdict—irresponsibility in one sphere of life was contagious to all others. "Moreover," he remarked, "property is the pivotal point on which is balanced the whole moral structure of society." He looked to see if the court reporters had taken this last down, and they had, and he was pleased.

The jury filed out and almost instantly filed back in.

"Guilty," said the foreman.

"Seven years," said the judge.

Shortly after the trial Polly Patch left Lady Bissop's employ. The judge arrived home from sitting on a commission inquiring into reform of the abortion laws—he took the view that abortion should remain a matter for the state rather than the individual parent, and be in general disallowed, on the grounds that white middle-class babies were at a premium, and these were the ones most frequently lost to the surgeon's knife—and found his wife in tears.

"She's gone," she said. "Polly Patch has gone! A chauffeured car came to take her away. She wouldn't even take her wages." "She wasn't entitled to any," said the judge automatically, "if she left without notice," but he wept, too, and so did the children, and all clung together in their grief, achieving a closeness not normally theirs, but to be remembered as long as they lived.

"I think she was sent by heaven," said Maureen Bissop.

"Or hell," said the judge. "Sometimes I think that hell is kinder than heaven." He had begun to doubt God's essential goodness.

The judge was presently able to move out of criminal law into tax litigation; this made his sexual life with his wife calmer, even ordinary. He stopped filling his children's mouths with sand and so forth when they annoyed him, feeling that Polly Patch would not have liked it, and that perhaps, in the great balance of life, their shock and discomfort weighed heavier than his convenience. Lady Bissop and he even had a little girl whom he insisted on calling Polly—but who fortunately was blessed with such good looks as her namesake was not—a cheerful little thing who livened the household considerably. It was in her honor that Lady Bissop abandoned the bold colors of her earlier choice, and took to gentle, tiny floral designs, which had considerable charm.

**24** Mary Fisher lives in the High Tower and considers the nature of loss, and longing. She still tells lies to herself; it is her nature. She believes that the rain falls because she is sad, that storms rage because she is consumed by unsatisfied lust and the crops fail because she is lonely. It has been the worst summer for fifty years and she is not at all surprised.

It is my opinion that Mary Fisher does not suffer as other people suffer. What she feels now is petulance. She is bothered by having too much of what she doesn't want—her mother and the two children—and too little of what she does want—Bobbo, sex, adoration, and entertainment.

Mary Fisher lives in the High Tower and finds that food has no taste and the sun has no warmth, and is surprised.

Mary Fisher should know better. She was brought up in the gutter by a part-time whore of a mother, but she has wiped all that from her mind. Still she pretends the world is not as it is, and passes the error on. She will not learn: she will not remember. She has started another novel, *The Gates of Desire*.

Bobbo builds a new life in the prison library and suffers from depression, and loss of liberty, and the absence of Mary Fisher, or that part of her he remembers most clearly, the bit where the legs split off from the body. Sometimes, I imagine, he tries to think of her face. But Mary Fisher's features are so regular and so perfect they are hard to remember. She is all women because she is no woman.

Well, time passes: little by little all things proceed to the end I have appointed for them. I do not put my trust in fate, nor my faith in God. I will be what I want, not what He ordained. I will mold a new image for myself out of the earth of my creation. I will defy my Maker, and remake myself.

I cast off the chains that bound me down, of habit, custom, and sexual aspiration; home, family, friends—all the objects of natural affection. Not until then could I be free, and could I begin.

The extraction of so many of my teeth was the first step to the New Me. The dentist did not in fact remove them all: he filed every alternate tooth down to a point just below the gum line. The pain of the filing was intense: worse than any the judge inflicted. And the general day-to-day grinding and pounding of what was left was not pleasant—but then neither was living with the judge.

*Il faut souffrir,* as I pointed out to him, in order to get what you want. The more you want the more you suffer. If you want everything you must suffer everything. The people in a really lamentable state, of course, are the ones who suffer at random, and gain nothing. Lady Bissop is a case in point.

I wanted Bobbo to receive a long sentence because my sentence was long. I wanted him put on ice, as it were, until I was ready for him.

Sometimes I wonder how it is that I can be so indifferent to the mental discomfort—I won't say suffering, because Bobbo is warm and fed, and has no responsibilities—of a man who fathered my children, and who has spent so much time inside my body. The very fact that I wonder disturbs me. I am not all she-devil. A she-devil has no memory of the past—she is born afresh every morning. She deals with the feelings of today, not yesterday, and she is free. There is a little bit of me left, still woman.

A she-devil is supremely happy: she is inoculated against the pain of memory. At the moment of her transfiguration, from woman to nonwoman, she performs the act herself. She thrusts the long, sharp needle of recollection through the living flesh into the heart, burning it out. The pain is wild and fierce for a time, but presently there's none.

I sing a hymn to the death of love and the end of pain.

Look how Mary Fisher squirms and wriggles on the pin of remembered bliss. How she hurts! Moreover, she hears all too clearly what the villagers say. She has no one now to stop her ears with endearments and enticements and the lovely flatteries of the flesh. She hears more, in fact, than there is to hear.

Down in the village, or so Mary Fisher believes, they say that the owner of the High Tower is willfully childless—that is to say selfish, that is to say hardly a woman at all. They say she is brutal to her poor mother, and keeps her locked in a room. They say she is cruel to her lover's children; a really vicious stepmother. They say she is a marriage-breaker. Some say she drove her lover's wife to suicide, for didn't the poor woman disappear? They say that in her greed and wickedness Mary Fisher drove her lover to crime, and then, either hot with lust for her manservant, or angered because her lover, sickened by her nature, wouldn't marry her, betrayed him: failed to save him from prison.

They say it is people like Mary Fisher who move into a community and put property prices up so that local people can no longer afford to live in their own village.

Guilt, in fact, speaks into Mary Fisher's ears: she mistakes the voice for that of the villagers but she is wrong. What she hears is herself talking to herself.

And sometimes Andy and Nicola say things that indicate that they, too, think badly of her.

"If you can't say anything pleasant," she says, "don't say anything at all." But Andy and Nicola take no notice. They always do the opposite of what Mary Fisher wants. They don't like her. She does not like them. But they have lost their mother and their father and there is nowhere else for them to go, and they are Bobbo's flesh and blood, and Mary Fisher loves Bobbo, or thinks she does, with so much spirit and in such concentrated essence it doesn't matter much whether he's there in the flesh or not.

Well, sometimes Mary Fisher thinks that. Only at night, going to sleep, or in the morning, waking, when the itch of unsatisfied flesh—not quite a pain, not quite unendurable, simply uncurable—makes itself known, does she think, Yes, the only thing that matters is Bobbo's presence with her, here and now. Perhaps what she feels is lust, not love?

Garcia is triumphant. He is in love, or lust, and not with Mary Fisher. He has made the object of his love, or lust, one of the village girls, pregnant, and has brought her home to the High Tower to live. Someone, probably Garcia's love, has been stealing Mary Fisher's jewelry. All her lovely pieces, mementos of delicate passion, relics of fine acts of sexual discrimination, pre-Bobbo, have vanished. The girl, Joan, walks insolently about the High Tower, with her belly swelling, snickering in corners with Nicola, making Mary Fisher feel inferior, hardly a woman at all, because she never had a baby, and now, she realizes, never will.

Once Mary Fisher thought she was blessed in her childlessness, spared the degradation, the ordinariness, the pointlessness of motherhood: no more. She needs something, anything.

Her flesh and her soul call out to Bobbo. She can write to him once a month, and he to her, likewise. She writes about love, with the practiced skill at her command, and he writes back strange halting letters about the weather or the prison food, and expressing anxiety about the dog Harness, and the cat Mercy, and the children's welfare.

Mary Fisher tries to get Bobbo's parents to look after Nicola and Andy, but Angus and Brenda cannot, and will not. They live in hotels, they explain, not homes. They cannot take pets or children into their lives. Once was enough with Bobbo, and look how he turned out! Besides, they lay Bobbo's downfall at Mary Fisher's door, and have no desire to do her a good turn.

But they do come to visit occasionally, and Mary Fisher is glad of the company. What she has come to!

"Such a wonderful place for children!" says Brenda. She is dressed in mauves and greens, and is less silky and more gauzy than usual, as if to underline her impracticality, her flyaway nature. "All this space! A crime not to fill it! And Nicola and Andy are so happy here. They look very well, considering."

Considering, she means, their misfortunes, brought upon them by Mary Fisher. She, Brenda, brings the children bubble gum, which blows up and bursts pinkly over noses and cheeks and in hair, and when finally chewed to nonelastic is stuck under the ridges of tables and beds, for strangers to come across unexpectedly.

"Poor little mites," says Brenda, looking up at her great hulking pair of grandchildren. They accept the bubble gum partly in recognition of her kindness, partly to annoy Mary Fisher, and partly because, although on the brink of maturity, they long to stay children. They have a memory of paradise, a golden age, at 19 Nightbird Drive. It makes them sulky and morose. Neither is doing well at school.

Nicola bursts a bubble-gum balloon in a Doberman's ear, and the great beast snaps at her nose and she has to have sixteen stitches to join the torn flesh and seal the grated bone. Nicola cries for her lost mother for the first and last time.

Mary Fisher sees Andy looking at her, sometimes, with lustful and predatory eyes. He is much too young to look like that at anyone, let alone the woman his father loves, but what can she do? She'd send them both to boarding school, but she knows they'd just come back, as her mother used to from the nursing homes. They say that's what they'll do, and she believes them. Bobbo does not want them to visit him in prison.

"Let them forget me," he says.

Mary Fisher fears what he means is let him forget them.

Old Mrs. Fisher is bedridden and incontinent and on huge doses of Valium. Occasionally she starts up and says, "What have I come to? A nest of criminals! She's the one who ought to be in jail!" and Mary Fisher is so low she cries, and feels that in all the world she has no one, no one.

"What about us?" ask Andy and Nicola, following Mary Fisher with their eyes wherever she goes. Sometimes she feels she's living in a horror movie.

Mary Fisher begs Angus and Brenda at least to take Harness the dog, for Bobbo's sake, but they won't.

"Best thing to do is to get the poor beast put to sleep," says Angus. "A dog's no good without its master; like that, they were." And he uses his fingers to show the intertwining of man and dog.

But Mary Fisher can't have the dog put to sleep. Once she could, now she can't. She knows too much: she knows what Harness would feel. I could murder a dozen dogs with impunity, if it was in my interests. I started with the guinea pig, and now look! I am a she-devil. I wouldn't be surprised if I wasn't the second coming, this time in female form; what the world has been waiting for. Perhaps as Jesus did in his day for men, so I do now, for women. He offered the stony path to heaven: I offer the motorway to hell. I bring suffering and self-knowledge (the two go together) for others and salvation for myself. Each woman for herself, I cry. If I'm nailed to the cross of my own convenience I'll put up with it. I just want my own way, and by Satan I'll have it.

She-devils have many names, and an infinite capacity for interfering in other people's lives.

**25** Ruth, having achieved her purpose in the judge's house, and still having a month or so of dental surgery to undergo, looked for lodgings in Bradwell Park, a place where she felt she could safely achieve anonymity. Many people of odd size, shape, and appearance lived here and few bothered to turn their heads as she went by. Bradwell Park was deep in the western suburbs, an extensive, depressed, and featureless section of the city. Here the poor lived.

Ruth had $2,563,072.45 on deposit in a Swiss bank, but preferred to live simply and cheaply for the time being. The rich are noticeable, the poor anonymous: a dull gray cloak of invisibility flung over their lives. And Ruth did not want to draw the attention of the police or the fiscal authorities to herself before the time was ripe. And in Bradwell Park, moreover, she was unlikely to meet anyone from Eden Grove who'd say, "Why, isn't it Bobbo's wife? Fancy seeing you!"

Bradwell Park and Eden Grove, where Ruth had lived in her other life, were both defined as suburbs, but were very different places. In Bradwell Park men and women lived higgledy-piggledy: in Eden Grove they contained themselves in neat, fenced squares. There were more women than men in Bradwell Park, fewer garages for fewer cars, and only one communal swimming pool, so highly chlorinated it could cause temporary blindness. In Bradwell Park lived people who earned less than they would like to earn, and women who were trapped by necessity rather than by the complexity of their desires, but who at least had the consolation of knowing that their discontent was not mere restlessness and ingratitude, but justified.

Ruth stood outside the Social Security office for a time until someone suitable came out: a young woman in her late teens, pregnant, with two small children at her heels, pushing her shopping in their stroller. She was pretty, pasty-faced, and distracted. She waited at the bus stop: when the bus came Ruth helped her on board with the children, the stroller, and the shopping—while the conductor stood by—and then sat beside her and fell into casual conversation.

The girl's name was Vickie. Martha was three and Paul was two. No, she had no husband, and had never had one.

"I'm looking for lodgings," said Ruth. "Do you know anywhere?"

Vickie didn't.

"I suppose there isn't a corner in your house?" said Ruth. "In exchange for baby-sitting and a little housework? And I could pay a little something toward the rent. No need to tell Social Security!"

The prospect of extra money and a little help overcame Vickie's quite justifiable fear that the house she lived in was unsuitable for anyone with any choice in the matter, and presently Ruth was installed in Vickie's back room, sleeping on a camp bed which broke the first time she lay upon it. The room was generally unused because it was dark, dank, and cold, but Ruth brightened it with posters and hung burlap on the walls to keep back the crumbling plaster.

"How lucky you are to be tall," said Vickie. "You don't have to use a stepladder. That's why I've never gotten around to it: I don't have one. That, and the cost of the burlap. And I don't see why I should do it, anyway. It's the landlord's job."

Vickie had left school when she was sixteen, found there were no jobs to be had, and gone on welfare. Leisure was minimally less boring than any job that would have been available to her but was perhaps even more enervating. Vickie, as she told Ruth, had suffered from asthma when a child and her lungs were certifiably weak, so the jobs that were open to her contemporaries in Bradwell Park—working in the big laundry and dry-cleaning centers that served large areas of the city—were not open to her. Constant exposure to steam and the vapors of dry-cleaning fluids quickly destroy even the youngest and healthiest lungs, so Vickie was fortunate that her disability had gone on file, and her benefit allowances were not progressively cut in order to prompt her to take such work as was available locally, however disagreeable.

*"Nil bastardi carborundum,"* said Vickie, laughing bitterly. Or, Don't let the bastards grind you down. She'd picked up the phrase from a passing college lover.

At the age of eighteen Vickie had felt quite sorry for herself and thought that to give her life a purpose and a meaning she should have babies, and set about achieving this ambition. It is always important to have someone to love, as well as something to do. Once she had a baby, the Welfare Department paid her rent and gave her vouchers for electricity and food, and if she argued enough, War on Want would pay her gas bill and her television rental and keep her washing machine in order. But it was hard work getting around from department to department, encumbered as she was by her two small children. One way and another, she would have enough for the children's breakfast, but not for their supper, and so forth. In return, the state demanded respect and gratitude and not—as any Bradwell Park husband would—merely payment in kind, of the flesh. Sex in Bradwell

Park was regarded as a bargaining ploy, rarely seen as a source of mutual pleasure or spiritual refreshment, and the notion of partnership between man and wife was generally abhorrent to both sexes.

Vickie wriggled and protested and insulted and derided the state, her provider, in much the same way that wives will insult and deride the husbands who provide for them, care for them, love them. Vickie's second baby, Paul, was born to a father recognizably his, who stayed for six months after the birth, only to go out one evening to buy a packet of cigarettes, never to reappear.

"Don't worry," the sister at the clinic had said to the weeping Vickie. "He hasn't been run over or swept up by a flying saucer. He's all right. He'll turn up in a month or so living with someone just around the corner. It happens all the time around here. It's the breakup of the social fabric, I'm told."

"But he loved me. Surely he'd have told me!"

"I expect he didn't want to upset you. And little Paul isn't the easiest baby and some men just don't like acting father to a child who isn't their own. And how *is* little Martha? Did the impetigo go?"

"It's back," Vickie had complained. "It's all his fault. Little Martha loved him! How could a man treat a little child like that? She's so upset!"

"Vickie," said the sister sadly, "either you have your children inside the system devised by society for the protection of women and children, namely marriage, or you live outside it and put up with the consequences."

"*Nil bastardi carborundum*," muttered Vickie.

Another man soon moved into the space left by Paul's father—nature abhors an empty bed—and stayed for three months, before moving on to a less child-encumbered woman; leaving Vickie pregnant.

And thus Ruth had found her.

Sales of Mary Fisher's books were good in Bradwell Park. The women bought them, while the men bought comics such as *The Grinning Skull* and *Monster Man* and all felt temporarily better. Video machines were popular, and sex-and-violence films shown as family entertainment within the home, in a way inconceivable in Eden Grove.

"Why can I never find true love?" Vickie asked Ruth, while Ruth swept through her house, sweeping up orange peel, disposing of old clothes, washing curtains that had never been washed, finding bedspreads and cot covers that had never been used, getting rid of grease and despondency, which so often go together.

"Because you're always pregnant," said Ruth to Vickie.

But there you are! Some women are born to pregnancy, in spite of pill, coil, diaphragm, or God's calendar. And why should a man bother to thwart a fecund woman, when pregnancy seems to be what she wants, and the state provides? Someone to love, something to do—it's all any of us want.

Ruth and Vickie would laugh about it, as they sat in front of the gas fire on winter nights. Damp diapers hung sensibly around—there was no money for a dryer, but would be soon, out of Ruth's contribution to the rent. What a life! Vickie had sometimes vaguely hoped that either Martha or Paul would be out of diapers before the new baby was born, but she did little to realize the hope. Well, what can you do about infant kidneys, toddlers' bladders? They develop in their own time and at the clinic they say toilet training is useless, and even traumatic for the child. And the cold! Ruth sometimes had to wear three pairs of Paul's father's socks—he had left all his clothes behind in his attempt to save Vickie's feelings. He'd lately been sighted, wheeling a baby carriage out shopping on a Saturday afternoon.

The sister explained it.

"There are some men, my dear, who love the whole process of pregnancy, birth, and new babies, and lose interest as the child grows older. Some women are like that, too. Why should such a nature be the prerogative of women? You can't have it all ways!"

Vickie had lived in a state of discontent and general surprise that saucepans should be so thin, beds so broken, debts so worrying, and the children not just prone to sore throats and chilblains, but so obstreperous. It was not what she had meant at all. This was not motherhood, as she had dreamed of it, but she had a valiant nature and kept trying. Ruth, by living in the back room, paid for peanut butter and jelly to spread on the children's bread, and condensed milk to put in her coffee, not to mention twenty Marlboros a day and the bus fares to the clinic to receive the emotional counseling and contraceptive advice that might prevent the birth of the child after next—but that child, the fourth, might be a genius, might be the perfect child to which Vickie might be the perfect mother! (Morning sickness had already disappointed her in the third.) Had Ruth thought of that, asked Vickie, half-laughing, half-crying? Wasn't contraception as wicked as abortion? It certainly *felt* so, to her. And what did Vickie have to go by in her life but feelings?

"Yes, I had thought of that," said Ruth. "The possible loss of a genius. But it's rather like winning the lottery, isn't it? Simply not likely."

There was, Ruth noticed, working in the Bradwell Park Catholic Mission opposite the Social Security offices, and offering free day-care service and refreshments to young mothers, a certain Father Ferguson. When Vickie stopped for a cup of tea, a chat, and a general sit-down, it would be Father Ferguson who chatted. Vickie loved him. Father Ferguson said that Vickie was very wise and a daughter of God, and that the clinic, who kept recommending terminations and sterilizations, was very wrong, and indeed wicked. Women's happiness and fulfillment lay in increasing the flow of souls to God. Father Ferguson came calling on Vickie one day and Ruth asked him in. Vickie was out.

He looked around the neat and clean, though sparsely furnished, room and said, "There's a great difference here. I suppose that's your doing?"

"It is," said Ruth.

"I'm in need of a housekeeper," he said.

"So is Vickie," observed Ruth.

"Vickie can manage," he said. "She only has the children to think about. And at least I'd pay you."

Ruth said she'd bear it in mind.

He was a lean, lithe, ascetic man, a natural celebate. He waded through a sea of rampant female flesh, of bosoms and bellies and underarm smells and never turned back or looked to shore. His ears were finely tuned to the music of the spheres and daily assaulted by the seagull shrieks, the laughter and hysteria of womanhood, yet he never blocked them.

Ruth left Vickie's house one Thursday morning, when the frost was thick on the ground, to keep a final appointment with Mr.

Firth, her dentist. She went to him using the name of Georgiana Tilling. The journey took two and a half hours. One of the features of the western suburbs is its lack of public transport, and the high cost of what small service there is. Ruth was obliged to walk half a mile uphill to the nearest bus stop, travel a mile and a half by bus to the nearest station, and, once on the train, change twice before reaching her destination, which was in that central part of the city where the wealthiest and most successful doctors and dentists had their offices.

Little tropical fish swam in Mr. Firth's examination room, and moving patterns played upon the wall in front of his patient's eyes. He used acupuncture and hypnotism to alleviate dental pains. Mr. Firth was lantern-jawed, benign, and in his caring prime.

Ruth lay reclined in his new chair and found it was not quite long enough for comfort. Mr. Firth examined Ruth's mouth.

"This is excellent, Miss Tilling," he said. "You have a remarkable healing capacity: a real gift for recuperation. Your jaw will now stand a good three-inch trim; one inch is usually the most that is contemplated, but new developments in laser technology and microsurgery make many things possible that never were so before. You will be making facial history! Of course, to this end, we have had to extract three times as many teeth as we usually do to reduce the dental arch proportionately. I think it has hurt me more than it hurt you—to extract such healthy, powerful, stubborn teeth in the interest of appearance rather than health is not what a dentist likes to do. However, the world moves on, whether we like it or not. I hope you will agree with me that acupuncture is a wonderfully safe and effective means of pain control."

"Igh hag no effeg on me ath all," said Ruth, and after she had spat a little into the swirling mauve water in the steel basin, "as you know perfectly well."

Mr. Firth allowed himself a few more remarks about the anti-social nature of cosmetic surgery inasmuch as it took up the time and skill of highly trained practitioners and on the vanity and frivolity of those women who sought it, then called in his long-legged blond receptionist to take Ruth's money. Ruth paid Mr. Firth $1,761, which included $11 to the glowing little hygienist who had done the final smoothing down of the sharp stumps and the fitting of the temporary crowns. Ruth told Mr. Firth she would have her stumps permanently crowned elsewhere.

"Do as you think fit," he said. "I can't stop you. But you won't get anyone to do it honestly. They'll take your money and give you pearly little teeth which won't match your character and will look ridiculous."

"Then I shall change my character to fit the teeth," said Ruth. "Good day!"

Ruth then went to keep her appointment with Mr. Roche, the leading surgeon in the city. His specialty was remodeling noses. He had started as a gynecologist but had found the burden of responsibility—the giving and taking away of life itself—too onerous. Cosmetic surgery, by comparison, was simple and gratifying.

Or so he had thought. But Ruth had arrived with wide ranging, complex, and even hazardous cosmetic requirements. He therefore turned to his protégé, Mr. Carl Ghengis, for help. Both men were present when Ruth was shown into the consulting room.

Mr. Ghengis was in his late forties, a decade younger than Mr. Roche, but a high flyer. He had started life as a garage mechanic; had his appendix removed in his midtwenties, realized that the human body was no more than a machine, and moved into medicine, beginning his career with false degrees from a nonexistent university and proving so brilliant a doctor that this initial shortcoming, even upon revelation by a spiteful nurse, had been overlooked.

He had worked for some years as Mr. Roche's assistant, then moved on to California, when the boom in genetic engineering began. He still from time to time visited Mr. Roche and took on those few patients whose troubles baffled, worried, or frightened his mentor, and who had reasonable financial means. Reasonable, to those used to dealing with multimillionaires, means a great deal of wealth indeed. Mr. Carl Ghengis was dashing, silky of skin and manner, eager-looking, and of slim build. He had soft and gentle eyes and a vaguely dusky complexion. His father was an American, his mother a Goan. He moved like a young man, almost on tiptoe, as if forever poised for flight. His fingers were pale and long and strong, and flattened at the end, as is a scalpel.

He took Ruth's large hands in his, smoothed them and studied them, as a mother might a child's, then looked up at her. "We can change everything but the hands," he said. "They remain as evidence of our heredity and our past."

"Then I shall wear gloves," said Ruth impatiently. The possession of much money had made her bold and brisk, and easily irritated.

"Tell me," he said, for he believed in the power of intimacy, "what is it you *really* want?"

"I want to look up to men," she said, better-humored already, and she laughed her grating, uncomfortable laugh. "That's what I want."

You could tighten the vocal chords, he thought, alter the resonance of the voice box and change the laugh. He took nothing for granted. He thought the human body was an imperfect instrument at the best of times, which should be tuned and trimmed until it fitted the soul. Once he himself had had hammer toes; now he had little plastic splints running alongside the bone, keeping them straight, and his toes were sightly by the swimming pool and more in keeping with his nature. His mother had been poor, he'd worn his elder brother's shoes: it had done him no good.

Mr. Ghengis and Mr. Roche stripped, weighed, photographed, and studied Ruth from many angles.

"Better too much than too little!" joked Mr. Ghengis to Mr. Roche. "Easier to abstract than to add. Do you think she'll go putrid?"

"Shouldn't think so," said Mr. Roche. "The gums have healed beautifully. See?"

They peered into her mouth as if she were a horse and they were trying to guess its age.

"I'd love to have a try at the nose all the same," said Mr. Roche. "I'll fly you out for the nose," said Mr. Ghengis kindly.

"You can't do it here?" Mr. Roche seemed surprised. "She'll have to go abroad?"

"My clinic," said Mr. Ghengis, "in the Californian desert."

"I could do with a holiday myself," said Mr. Roche, looking out at the city rain. He returned his attention to the patient. "Heartbeat's very slow. Almost out of the normal range."

"Better too slow than too fast."

"And a remarkably low blood pressure," Mr. Roche added.

"All to the good," said Mr. Ghengis. "What isn't good is the layer of blubber."

"Can't you just cut that away, too?" asked Mr. Roche.

"Not in too great an area," said Mr. Ghengis. "Better for her to lose the weight now than afterward, and to do it naturally."

"How much weight?" asked Mr. Roche.

Mr. Ghengis turned to Ruth, who was pulling on her clothes behind the screen. The screen barely reached shoulder height. "When you've lost forty pounds," he said, "we'll start."

Living with Vickie had been making Ruth fatter day by day. The foods the household could afford to buy were rich in carbohydrates, and the boredom imposed by poverty led the two women to eat constant snacks and steal scraps from the children's plates. Sweet coffee and biscuits got them through the long mornings, sweet tea and buns through the dreary afternoons.

Ruth went home to Vickie and told her that she no longer required the back room.

"But I'm pregnant," wailed Vickie, as if this gave her special rights in the world.

"You always will be," said Ruth, sadly, packing her few large belongings. The bed here was too short, but whenever had a bed not been so? The bed linen was thin and sad and, however frequently washed, remained stained with bright splotches where the children had left the tops off felt-tip pens.

"What's to become of me?" moaned Vickie, and Martha and Paul hung around Ruth's large ankles, but she shook them off easily enough. Andy and Nicola had clung with sharper claws. Sometimes Ruth dreamed of her children, and they reached up their little arms to her, but she knew well enough, on waking, that their arms were no longer little.

"If I were you," said Ruth, "I would sell the unborn baby, in advance, for a large sum, to adoptive parents. And of course Paul and Martha can also be sold. There are many rich people in the world only too anxious to adopt pretty, healthy white children. By so doing you will be giving your children a better start in the world, ensuring them a longer life, more interesting friends, more beautiful sexual partners, and a much more rewarding life in general than if you condemn them to scrape away down here with you, at the bottom of the world's barrel. Sell them!"

"But I love them!" cried Vickie, in shock.

"But so would their adoptive parents. Little creatures with big eyes bring out caring instincts in almost anything alive. If a baby crocodile so much as whinnies the entire man-eating tribe turns up to find out what's the matter. And just think, Vickie, you could have a holiday on the proceeds!"

"But they'd miss me. They'd suffer. What about 'the bond'?"

There was much talk of "the bond" down at the clinic and a good deal done to foster it. It was less taxing on welfare funds to have mothers looking after their own progeny than leaving the state to do it.

"What about their impetigo?" asked Ruth. "What about their chilblains, their dripping noses?"

Vickie, taking offense at the notion of impetigo, said that if Ruth were going she'd better go at once, and she'd always eaten more than her share anyway, and done less cleaning than her share, but Vickie had held her tongue about it until now.

"And what about sisterhood?" demanded Vickie. "You're always saying women should stick together. Now look at you!"

Ruth shrugged. Vickie followed Ruth to the door.

"You're disgusting," she said. "You're immoral, heartless, and disgusting! I thank God I'm not like you. You think money equals happiness. It doesn't. How could I possibly exchange my children, the meaning of my life, for money?"

Vickie ran after Ruth as she got to the gate.

"Supposing I was to do anything so awful," said Vickie, "supposing I did want to sell the children, how would I go about it?"

Ruth, who by now knew the ins and outs of the city, the cunning ways of the multitude that lived on the underside, told her. Then she went to visit Father Ferguson. She knew him to be an abstemious man, and if she was to lose forty pounds she would need to be in a house where the food was meager and the living lean.

**26** Mary Fisher has very little money in the bank, and only the High Tower to her name. Her other houses have been sold to defray Bobbo's legal expenses. The tax authorities, angry with Bobbo and by proxy with Mary Fisher, have decided she owes them very large sums indeed for tax underpaid in previous years. It is Judge Bissop who ratifies their demands, rejecting Mary Fisher's astonished appeal. Now she has yet more legal fees to pay. Her royalties for years to come are confiscated. *The Gates of Desire* is nearly finished. She has hopes of it. She has to have some hope, somewhere. People do.

Mary Fisher wakes alone, writhing and sobbing in her silken sheets. She wants no one else but Bobbo, and there is no one else to want, in any case. Garcia makes love to Joan the village girl in all the stray corners of the house. Mary Fisher remonstrates.

"I'll do as I please," says Garcia. "And who are you to object? There was a time you couldn't even bother to answer the telephone, you were so hard at it, and didn't care who knew!"

Mary Fisher is frightened of Garcia, who knows too much and could always tell, though what and to whom she can scarcely remember. All she knows is that she has to keep him happy.

She sinks into sloth: the pangs of unsatisfied lust grow less, or perhaps she is just used to them. She eats ravioli out of cans, and bags of sticky candies, and grows thick around the middle. She cannot remember Bobbo's face, any more than he can remember hers. She remembers love, though, and still writes about it. She finishes *The Gates of Desire*. Her publishers are pleased. Perhaps she will soon be rich again? Perhaps!

Mary Fisher tosses and yearns and waits to be filled, and writes about love. Her lies are worse because now she knows they are lies. She remembers her past: she understands what she is.

Mary Fisher did a wicked thing: she set herself up in a high building on the edge of a high cliff and sent a new light beaming out into the darkness. The light was treacherous; it spoke of clear water and faith and life when in fact there were rocks and dark and storms out there, and even death, and mariners should not be lulled but must be warned. It is not just for myself that I look for vengeance.

I can, I suppose, in the end, forgive Mary Fisher for many things. It was in the name of love that she did what she did, before I brought her to the understanding of what love is; or indeed, of what it is to be abandoned by a husband, to be condemned to a living death of humiliation, anxiety, and woe. I daresay I might have done the same myself, had I stood in her little size 4 shoes. But I don't forgive her novels. She-devils are allowed to be petulant.

Garcia rings to ask if he should get Harness put to sleep. He cannot get a clear answer from Mary Fisher, who is as inconsolable at Bobbo's absence as the dog. Harness, says Garcia, is now disturbed, incontinent, uncontrollable in traffic, and has taken to snatching the food from Mary Fisher's plate. Even the vet says there is nothing for him but merciful oblivion. What do I think?

"I think you must do as the vet suggests," say I. I cannot have Harness eating the food from Mary Fisher's plate. As she grows fat, I shall grow thin. That's the way it is.

Harness goes to the vet and does not return.

"Do you believe in God?" Mary Fisher asks Garcia.

"Of course I do!" he says.

"I used to," she says. "If only I could believe again. He was such a great consolation."

**27** Father Ferguson lived in the house next to his church, in a central area of the city where the new high-rises had not quite ousted the low stone brick buildings of the original town. He had been looking for a housekeeper for some time, but without success, for the house was large and cold and old and reputed to be haunted, and had no heating in winter or air-conditioning in summer. Father Ferguson did not like being too comfortable: he felt easier in his soul when slightly hungry, or too hot or too cold, or when he had toothache. He was a familiar sight in the city, a lean, white-haired, anguished figure, jogging to and from his church to the mission in Bradwell Park, morning and evening. It was a distance of five miles.

"There he goes!" his parishioners would say. "Isn't he a wonder! He has some odd notions for a priest, but a priest he is. Or else a saint!"

He was thirty-five. His hair had turned white when he was twenty-nine, when he had been obliged to deliver a baby to a drug-addicted mother in a derelict house. The baby was still-born. The mother rejoiced. He felt that the Devil was loose in the world.

Now he worked among the people. He was not popular with his ecumenical superiors, for he not only dabbled in political matters, but was unpredictable in his attitudes generally. He had been known to say in public that mouths must be filled before souls could be fed. He would lay the blame for sin at the state's door: he all but preached revolution while maintaining an almost absurd quietism in his personal affairs. He wanted the alcohol removed from the communion wine. He signed petitions that sought to outlaw nuclear warfare. His flock didn't like him either, although they felt duty bound to admire him, because he recommended celibacy for the unmarried, and abstinence for the married if they had decided against children. His flock thought he was mad: now there were antibiotics for social diseases, and contraception—and if necessary abortion—to prevent the accidental birth of children, what was he going on about? The welfare agencies thought he was wicked and hopelessly old-fashioned. As well blame the moon for lunacy!

Father Ferguson's church was falling down: no one would help him put it back up. Not just the house but the church was said to be haunted. Push open the door on a lonely night and sounds of music and the scent of incense and glimpses of bright color within could be heard and smelled and seen. Outside in the new big city the sound of traffic rose, day and night, never stopping: here in the old church lingered a memory of that other little world, long ago, which formed the new one, and left its poetry and its lingering customs to enrich it. People shivered and shook at the notion of a haunting that was divine, not diabolic. And in the house itself, they said, shadowy monks came and went, although certainly monks had never lived there.

Father Ferguson himself had never encountered either the ghostly service in his church or the ghostly monks in his house, and he was scathing about those who had.

"I believe in God," he said, "not ghosts. To believe in ghosts is an insult to the Almighty's creation!"

A property developer wanted the land on which the church and house stood to build yet another high-rise office block. Father Ferguson's masters, being in financial difficulties, would have liked the sale to go through, but Father Ferguson was obstinate. He was quoted in the local press as claiming that the Church was opting out of its responsibilities and abandoning the inner city to the Devil and the feminists (the property company was run by a woman) and turning its back upon the wretched of the world. Father Ferguson appeared to equate the Devil with capitalism, not communism, which was unfortunate. The matter reached the national press, and Father Ferguson made further headlines by suggesting that priests should be allowed to marry, that celibacy must be a matter of choice: that it was impossible to deal with God's breeding, teeming world properly as a half-man. The phrase was his: "Half-Man."

"Father Ferguson," said his masters, "do we hear you right? You recommend marriage without sex to the sheep and marriage with sex to the shepherd? Is this not inconsistency?"

"Not so inconsistent as Jesus," replied Father Ferguson, unabashed. "Blasting fig trees one day, turning cheeks the other."

Father Ferguson advertised weekly for a housekeeper. He needed one: he could not manage his clothes. He washed his shirts carefully but they did not come clean. He would rub the collar fabric thin, but still the dirt remained; he didn't understand it. Whenever he opened the great creaky wardrobe that had been his mother's, and a wedding present to her from her grandmother, and took out his trousers, there would be stains on them he could have sworn were not there the day before. Or perhaps he had put them away in a poor light, and taken them out in a strong one? Except the light in the house was never good. Once it had been surrounded by fields and flowers and trees, and the windows had let in more than enough; now the garages and the high-rises crowded in and sopped up God's light, leaving only dimness and fumes behind.

Sometimes he thought he was living in hell. The food in the refrigerator went bad. He did not understand it. Cold was supposed to preserve food. The inside of the cabinet was covered with a blackish, spotty mold. Perhaps he just left food in there for too long, forgetting the passage of time? He did not much appreciate or need food, but liked to have the odd square of cheese, or an egg for supper.

When Molly Wishant applied for the job of housekeeper it seemed to Father Ferguson that his problem was at last solved. She was a woman like no other. She could not possibly be seen by his parishioners as a source of erotic excitement. She was strong, well-spoken, and intelligent; she was escaping from nothing; and her reason for wanting the job—a desire to fill in time usefully while losing forty pounds, as a doctor had suggested she should—seemed to him unusual but acceptable. She would not become hysterical and claim the house was haunted. She was too somber a person to chatter at breakfast time; she did not wear a gold cross around her neck, in mockery of Our Savior's death, as so many did. She had facial moles from which hairs sprouted, so presumably lacked vanity and would not spend so much time in the bathroom, night or morning, as to inconvenience him. She would not run up the food bills. He did not think that the mere losing of weight would help the poor creature much: she would remain ungainly; but it was scarcely his business to point this out.

"Haven't I seen you somewhere before?" he asked.

"I used to help out at Vickie's house. You know, the pregnant girl with two children and no husband, down at Bradwell Park."

"I can't quite place her," he said. "There are so many like her."

"And will be more," said Molly Wishant, "if you go on telling them what you do."

"We are all God's children," he said, startled.

188

He hoped she did not feel the cold, that she would not waste the electric fires unnecessarily. She said she imagined her work would keep her warm. That was on the first day of her employment. She slept in one of the attic rooms, where plaster flaked from the ceiling whenever a truck went by in the street below. The bed was wire mesh hung from an iron frame, and the mattress old, old horsehair.

After a week Molly mentioned that Father Ferguson's shirts needed replacing. Father Ferguson replied that they were only ten years old and when she said that was quite old, for a shirt, he said that his father's had lasted twenty, so she agreed to make do. She took fabric from the bottom hems and patched underneath the arm. The priest's collars were detachable; he had been left an extra dozen in an uncle's will: they were lasting rather better than the shirts.

"God looks after his own," said Father Ferguson.

Presently she asked for soap and hot water to help her with the laundry, and he said that in the seminary in Italy in which he had been trained washing was done with cold stream water and without soap. Molly pointed out that the water there may well have been softer, but that the city water was hard; but she agreed to use those new detergents that worked in cold water as well as in hot.

She investigated the stains on his trousers and found some kind of fungus life in the top of the wardrobe which exuded drops of sticky liquid from time to time; this she eradicated.

She put 100-watt bulbs in the sockets instead of the 40-watt bulbs he had taken for granted, and the monklike shadows were revealed for what they were: the long curtains in the hall flying up in the draft that came blustering down from the attic when the dining room fire was lit, casting vague shapes on the upstairs gallery. Father Ferguson worried about the expense of the stronger bulbs but she assured him the difference in price was minimal.

He believed her. She inspired trust. She lost fifteen pounds in the first month she worked for him. She seemed to know what she was about. She was lonely and he was sorry for her.

She would not clean his church. She laughed and said it would not be suitable for an unbeliever to do so. She said she didn't believe in God, but she did believe in the Devil. She'd met him only recently, and had had closer contact with him than was pleasant. He thought he would rather deal with someone who acknowledged the Devil than with those many who professed to believe in God, but who saw Him only in anthropomorphic terms. That is, who trivialized Him.

He told her about the rumors that the church was haunted, and she said no doubt the rumors had been put about by the property developers who wanted to buy the land.

He came to think, in the space of six weeks or so, that she was precious: a pearl among women. For someone so large she moved silently. He hoped she would never leave. He began to tempt her with little morsels of food—at first squares of cheese, and apples, but then he would drop by the corner store and bring home jam doughnuts and apple turnovers. Not cheap; but the faster she lost weight the sooner she would go.

He saw that perhaps life could be pleasant without being frivolous. He accepted a bottle of sherry as a gift from one of the parishioners—a woman who, he later discovered, had given out her three children, two born and one unborn, for adoption. They had gone to good Christian families, albeit in the Lebanon. He called Molly down from her attic to help him drink it. His deep eyes flashed with a softer fire, and hers glittered redly. Outside the juggernauts rumbled by, and china clinked and lamps trembled, as if in an earthquake. It was never quite dark or quiet in the house, no matter how ancient the spirits within it.

"What was the woman's name?" asked Molly.

"Vickie, I think," said Father Ferguson, and Molly raised her glass.

"How much did she get for them?" she asked.

"Not even in Bradwell Park," said the Father, "do women sell their children for money!"

"Then they should start," said Molly.

They drank the entire bottle of sherry between them.

"Jesus turned water to wine," said Molly. "He can't have thought so badly of it."

"True," said Father Ferguson, and opened another bottle, which Molly happened to have by her. She wouldn't have any herself, pointing out that she was on a diet, so he was obliged to drink it all himself.

"Otherwise," said Molly, "it will go bad."

Father Ferguson had recently received a letter from his bishop asking him not to talk to the press without prior reference to his superiors, and suggesting that he should consider seriously whether he was guilty of the sin of arrogance.

"How can a man be humble and improve the world?" he asked.

"He can't," she said, thus giving him permission to sin. "Anyway, what's arrogance? It is a word. I am convinced; you are self-righteous; he is arrogant."

"How can a man stay celibate and understand his own nature?"

"He can't," she said, thus vindicating his frivolity.

He looked at her speculatively. Her two rows of crude white temporary teeth glowed an invitation.

"Will you marry me?" he asked.

She seemed startled.

"A civil marriage. Let them excommunicate me if they dare!"

As he spoke he thought he saw, out of the corner of his eye, a glimmer of movement up in the gallery; the cowled shapes of men passing to and fro, but he knew it could only be imagination, or the effects of alcohol, to which he was not accustomed.

"Did you see anything up there?" he asked.

"Not a thing." But she did. "Only the guilty see ghosts," she added, which he feared might be true.

She said she wouldn't marry him; she couldn't: she was married already, and so far as she was concerned marriage was once and once only and until death. As for anything else, any other way of arranging their lives to their mutual benefit, of increasing the funds of his self-knowledge, of making him a better priest, they would have to wait and see.

It had not occurred to Father Ferguson that he might meet resistance. That the clergy should marry, should have carnal knowledge with the opposite sex, it appeared, was one thing. Whether it *could* marry, could find anyone to bed, was another.

He began to see the complexities of life in the temporal world.

"You must understand," he said, "that for a man such as myself to lose my virginity to a woman such as you could not be construed as an act of impulse, let alone carnal turpitude. It would be chastely considered and implemented: the union of such unlikely flesh that it could only imply the sharing of my soul with yours. A supreme sacrifice."

"You are very persuasive," she said, allowing herself to be persuaded. There was quite a flurry at this among the ghostly visitors upstairs but she stared at them boldly, and they evaporated, melting into nothingness as he led her to his room.

Beside her in bed he felt warm and protected. He had the feeling that nothing of his had gone into her—which he had assumed would be the case in sexual congress—but that on the contrary something of her had gone into him.

They had bacon and eggs for breakfast, and toast and marmalade and coffee. He did not lament her extravagance. He would have forsworn jogging in Bradwell Park, but thought this might cause comment.

"You're either very bad for me, or very good for me," he said to Molly. She put on three pounds in weight, abandoning her diet for his sake, and after that he said only, "You are very good for me."

He knew he had changed because when presently he took confession from a woman who had been using contraceptives and whose husband had left her, he did not equate the sin with the consequence.

Usually in such circumstances he would say, "My child, your punishment has been on this earth, you are excused." Today he said briskly, "My child, I am sure our Heavenly Father would commend your good sense. You had the wit to know your husband would leave and took the responsibility of not bringing another mouth into the world for the state to feed. Peace be with you!"

And to a woman with five children, two subnormal, whose husband was a known drunkard, and violent, and insistent on his marital rights, he actually recommended a visit to the family planning clinic, forgetting his usual dictum of hard cases making bad law, a concept that worked as well in spiritual matters as in worldly ones.

He wanted to make an issue of it, of course. That was in his nature. He wanted to proclaim to the world that he was no longer a Half-Man; to claim his right to have intercourse with his housekeeper if he so decided. But Molly didn't want that.

"They'll only take photographs," she said. "I hate being photographed."

Well, he could understand her feelings.

In the third month Molly bought him new shirts and trousers out of parish funds—he had underspent for years on his personal needs. They shared Molly's room, and when it was cold they turned on all three bars of the electric heater. He began to understand, as he waited for night to fall and bedtime to come, why his flock was so insistent upon its sexual pleasures.

Molly said one night in the fourth month that the problem down in the western suburbs was not sex, which everyone knew was a sacrament, but love. Had he looked at the bookshops lately?

Did he understand that practically all the women who could read were buying romantic fiction? What hope did they have of ever reaching emotional maturity, let alone of gaining any kind of moral sense, if they read such rubbish?

"Worldly love is a shadow of the divine," said Father Ferguson. "I can hardly believe it is as dangerous as you say."

But he remembered what she said and at his next press conference—he had held them weekly since he received his bishop's letter begging prudence—he remarked that since these days the purveyors of fiction (in the absence of any moral guidance from a devitalized Church, and they knew his views on that) were the most powerful moral force in the land, they should be brought under Church control. Writers themselves, rather than their works, should be vetted for their sense of social responsibility. The writer would then have *carte blanche* to write what he or she wished. It was not a matter of censorship, but of self-censorship.

There was a gratifying uproar, and much protest from various writers' organizations, which made Father Ferguson feel he was really on to something. When you prodded the body politic and it squealed there was something nasty down there somewhere. But then his superiors rebuked him for interfering in matters that were nothing to do with the Church, and he let the whole question drop.

"You take too much notice of them," protested Molly.

"I must submit," he said. "I am still a priest."

"But you know the bureaucracy of the Church is venal. You have told me so often enough. They are politicians: you are divinely inspired, by God."

"My dear, I think you go a little too far." But he was pleased. All the same, he dropped the matter of the writers. He was beginning to feel quite soporific, almost lazy.

Molly had lost twenty-five pounds by the fifth month, and he had put on thirty. He could not have jogged to Bradwell Park had he tried, which of late he hadn't. He'd had a notice up in the Mission saying that advice and counseling was available at the clinic, and only went there once a week, by taxi, but felt guilty about it.

Molly had central heating installed in the house. He felt warmth pervading his bones: his mind no longer worked coolly and persistently but in rather agreeable sudden bursts. He was pleasantly and sensuously tired much of the time. The old oak furniture, the chests and bureaus and tables that had stood mellowing in dark corners for centuries, split their seams and warped their frames in the new hot, dry air. The ghostly visitors had gone forever, driven out by warmth and wine, and food and sex. They were never seen again.

Molly declared in the sixth month that perhaps Father Ferguson was by nature an administrator rather than a field-worker. Perhaps he could give up going to the Bradwell Park Mission altogether.

"But that would mean the Mission closing!"

"Your function, my dear, is to be a thorn in the side of the Church, for the Church's sake. Remember the parable of the talents?"

So the Mission closed and Father Ferguson was free of his guilt. He looked around for something to do.

"What about your Theory of Literary Responsibility?" said Molly.

"Too thorny a matter."

"But, my dear, you are the King of Thorns!"

He wrote persuasive letters to six leading writers of romantic fiction, from a list provided by Molly. Four replied, two did not. One of the latter was Mary Fisher.

"I think you should visit her," said Molly. "I think such defiance should not be allowed to pass. To ignore a letter from a man of the cloth? What insolence! It is almost blasphemy. It is an offense not just against you, but against the Church!"

"I love the way you're always on my side," he said. "I am so used to people arguing with me that to have someone agreeing with me is quite enchanting."

Father Ferguson put on his cassock, got into his new car, and drove off to the High Tower. Molly waved him good-bye.

**28** Mary Fisher lives in the High Tower and considers the nature of guilt, and responsibility. She weeps a great deal. It is a long time since she has been to bed with a man. She loves God, since there is no one else to love, and attributes to Him such qualities as Father Ferguson maintains he has.

She would love Father Ferguson, too, but he is a priest and she assumes that he is celibate; it has not occurred to her that he has a sexual nature. She approaches God through him, and that is all.

Old Mrs. Fisher rises up from her bed from time to time and shrieks, "Get that black crow out of here. Priests bring bad luck."

As if bad luck had not been surging all around Mary Fisher like the waves of the sea around the tower ever since Bobbo left his wife to live with her.

Father Ferguson says it is not bad luck but God's punishment for her sins. She is one of the fortunate, he says, much blessed by God. He punishes his favorites, it seems, in this world and not the next.

Father Ferguson has drunk his way through the best wines in Mary Fisher's cellar. Not that there were many bottles there.

Mary Fisher left wine-buying to men, and lately men have disappeared from her life.

It is a sign of the times: this running down, not just of people, but of things. Everywhere she looks it is the same. Garcia's baby by Joan was born with a hole in its heart. She cannot wish the baby spectacularly well, let alone its thieving mother, but she is upset by the spectacle of their distress. Father Ferguson soothes and explains the nature of God's love which somehow—she can never quite remember how—makes pain and suffering desirable.

Mary Fisher tells Father Ferguson about what she did to Bobbo's wife, and to Bobbo's children. She says she understands it was wicked. She says she knows that love is no justification for bad behavior. She wants to know how to be good.

"What you write is pernicious nonsense," says Father Ferguson bluntly. "You must stop. Then you will begin to be good."

This too! Father Ferguson explains how she has damaged the lives of a million readers: she has given them false expectations. She is personally responsible for much of the misery of the female multitude. Even the modern woman's taste for Valium he lays at her door. Mary Fisher's writing hand trembles and stops.

Father Ferguson says God is all-merciful: he will forgive the truly repentant, if they truly believe. Mary Fisher is desperate for forgiveness. She wants to truly believe, to be converted to Catholicism, and is.

Happy in her new faith, Mary Fisher grows plump and pretty again. She and Father Ferguson pray together, twice a week. He dines on Tuesdays and Thursdays, and stays over Thursday nights. She will use her name, her fame, her reputation, to save the world, and not add to its troubles. She starts a novel, *The*

*Pearly Gates of Love.* It is about a nun and her struggle for heavenly love. Her publishers are delighted.

Father Ferguson is less pleased. He explains to Mary Fisher that divine love and carnal love are not mutually exclusive.

"There is also a creative truth," says Mary Fisher, stronger in professional matters than in any other. "And that's what this novel needs. And if it's a sin, with the money I earn, who knows, perhaps I could build a chapel in the grounds."

That shocks him; at any rate he rebukes her. It is Thursday night. She goes to her room and weeps, leaving him alone. Garcia listens for the sound of Father Ferguson's following footsteps, climbing the stone stairs to Mary Fisher's white-and-silver bedroom, but hears nothing. He is glad: he has doubted her innocence. Mary Fisher is once again the object of his desire: he is disappointed in Joan, who steals and has produced an imperfect baby. He goes to Mary Fisher's room himself.

It is as if time, static for so long, hibernating, but now leaping and threshing, has swallowed its own tail, and she is back at the beginning. Perhaps she is cured of Bobbo, at last!

And then Father Ferguson is in the room, and Garcia is scurrying out of sight, for a priest is a priest.

Mary Fisher is appalled.

"Be of good cheer," says Father Ferguson, sitting casually upon the bed. "This is a small and venial sin compared to the rest."

But she doesn't believe him. She sees it all. She believes in love but practices lust: worships God but follows the Devil. She cannot even hold on to her love for Bobbo. She sees him as a merman, a man with a torso and tail and nothing between them.

She is humiliated. She, to whom Father Ferguson credited a soul, discovered humping and grunting like an animal, no better than the Doberman bitch.

Mary Fisher sees God disappearing from her life: becoming smaller and smaller, receding into infinity, leaving her with no forgiveness, only guilt.

"We must declare a truce," is all he says, "between good and evil, soul and body, spirit and the flesh. We must incorporate the bad within the good. The new God comes not to cast out sin but to welcome it. Only by knowing what we are can we achieve salvation."

And now he means to take away her guilt! It is all she has. It is the only order she can impose upon the chaos of her life.

"All things must change," says Father Ferguson. "Sin itself must change." But he looks like Chaucer's Pardoner, fleshy and greedy and happy, as if he has been there forever, waiting to exact his price. He enfolds her little form in his large and powerful arms, wraps his brown wool gown around her. It is a fine silky fabric, not rough-weave at all. "We must not deny our negative impulses," he says. "We are God's creation, every bit of us. We must glorify the flesh along with the soul."

Well, so much I've taught him. I wish the priest well and Mary Fisher bad. Garcia removes his eye from the keyhole: my vision of the scene is lost. All I know is that if she will with Garcia, she will with him, and if he will with me, he will with her, and why not, except I grudge Mary Fisher even ten minutes' happiness. That's all he'll give her.

But I like to tease Mary Fisher, too, to lob a little star of hope in front of her, in order to snatch it away. Why not? I remember making mushroom soup, and hoping for Bobbo's smile, and chicken vol-au-vents, in the hope of his approval, and chocolate mousse so that he would leave her and return to me. And he didn't. Let her take what's coming to her and put up with it. She has no option, anyway.

As for me, I must set out on the final stage of my journey. I admit I have hesitated, have found excuses to linger. But now I must move on. I have seen an insurance man pecking around the rectory: the same one who came to the fire at Nightbird Drive, to pick over the ashes. It is unlikely that he will recognize me as the same soft, distraught, poisoned, lumbering woman who watched her home go up in flames: now I am lean and tough and swift. All the same, prudence indicates that I should leave. Vultures have sharp eyes.

The fact remains there is stilll another fifteen pounds to lose. In flipping the coin of Father Ferguson's life, changing him from ascetic to hedonist, I had to pay a price. Now that he is away so much, I can start losing again. It's men who make women fat, that's obvious.

And I don't like it here anymore, anyway. Father Ferguson has sold out to the developers, of course: he is the darling of his bosses. Demolition men turn up from time to time to measure the house, as undertakers measure corpses for their coffins. I saw the house through its dying days, that's all, having brought about its death. It doesn't matter much. I dismissed its soul when I dismissed its ghosts.

Ruth, finding almost no difference now between her waist and her hips, telephoned Mr. Roche from a phone booth.

"You've lost forty pounds?"

"Possibly more."

He made an appointment with Ruth to see Mr. Ghengis the following week. The latter would fly over specially, he said, all the way from Los Angeles.

"You're an interesting case," said Mr. Roche.

"Why's that?"

"Such a challenge!"

"I wish to look what I want to look like, not what he wants me to look like," she warned.

There was a short silence.

"That may be very expensive," said Mr. Roche, eventually.

Ruth transferred her money in Switzerland to a Los Angeles bank: the transaction went through smoothly enough.

She went to a bookshop and bought a copy of *The Pearly Gates of Love*.

"How's it going?" she asked.

"Very badly," said the manageress. "Load of religious twaddle!"

And she called out to an assistant, "Alice, move the Fisher books off the shelves. Remember, shelf space is profit space!"

Ruth cut the picture of Mary Fisher from the book's dust jacket and dropped the book in the trash can. Mary Fisher stared up at the sky, in pretty, delicate profile, as if she had a hotline to God. She looked enchanting, and happy, and little. Ruth searched the bookshops for other novels by Mary Fisher, which might carry a full-length photograph, and was lucky enough to find one.

"Well!" said Mr. Ghengis, when he looked at the photographs. "Wow, even! But that's a real problem."

"Why so?" asked Ruth grimly.

"The hair's nothing, the face we can do—these are classic features we're looking at. The mouth will be tricky, but possible. When your jaw's trimmed the lipline will fall quite nicely into place. We work from the inside out as much as possible, of course. We can reshape the body quite dramatically—you *have* got thin, haven't you! How did you do that?"

"By keeping away from men," said Ruth.

"Not a very popular remedy with most of my patients! They'd rather have large slices cut off them any day—but, my dear, the proportion is going to look odd. This lady is at least six inches shorter than you."

"Then you must make tucks in my legs," she said. "I know it can be done."

It was a little while before he replied.

"Three inches from the femur is the most anyone has undertaken. It's easy enough to remove bone—you simply chop. But muscles, sinews, arteries, tendons all have to be equivalently looped, or shortened. It is not simple and not totally safe."

"I will accept the responsibility," said Ruth. "You give new hearts, new kidneys, new livers, and so forth: all I am asking you to do is take unnecessary stuff away."

"But in such quantity!"

"Modern surgical techniques improve year by year. You can use chip technology, microsurgery, lasers. Can't you?"

"A body remains a body," said Mr. Ghengis, "and a body scars if you open it up. You can even get keloid scarring: puckering and wrinkling. A terrible mess! If it happens, there is nothing we can do about it. And we can't take more than three inches from your femur. That is final."

"Then take some out of the shinbone."

"It's never been done."

"Then be the first. Or would you prefer to remove some of my vertebrae?"

"No!" He sounded panicky.

She smiled complacently. She felt she had won. So did he. He tried one last gambit:

"The other thing that occurs to the cosmetic surgeon," he said, "is that though you can change the body you cannot change the person. And little by little—this may sound mystical, but it is our experience—the body reshapes itself to fit the personality. And the personality of those who have the courage and will to seek cosmetic surgery may be handsome, but it isn't pretty. You are asking to be made pretty: trivial, if you will forgive me."

He had gone too far. He did not go on.

"I have an exceptionally adaptable personality," Ruth observed. "I have tried many ways of fitting myself to my original body, and the world into which I was born, and have failed. I am no revolutionary. Since I cannot change the world, I will change myself. I am quite sure I will settle happily enough into my new body."

"It will cost you millions of dollars. Is it worth it?"

"I have them. Yes."

"It will take years."

"I have them."

"I can stop you looking old, but you will *be* old."

"No. Age is what the observer sees, not what the observed feels."

He gave up. He agreed to take her into his clinic for, as he put it, extensive renovation. His assistant would be a Dr. Black. He would call in other specialists as required. He would be writing to her. In the meantime Ruth should go back to her normal life.

Some ten days later Ruth received a letter from Mr. Ghengis's clinic enumerating the processes she was to undergo and giving approximate prices. Detailed estimates were not practical, since healing processes varied from individual to individual; and, the implication was, surgeons never knew quite what they'd find inside the human body until they got there. The writing paper was of palest, tasteful mauve, and the words "Hermione Clinic" were embossed in gold at the top with a broad white flat clinical strip beneath. Ruth was reminded of the cover of one of Mary Fisher's novels—but given a medical seal of approval. The paper created hope and inspired confidence at the same time. It managed to be both romantic and scientific.

The Hermione Clinic meant to take back Ruth's jaw three inches, raise and fine the eyebrows, lower the hairline with a skin graft, and lift slack from beneath the skin and the epicanthic fold above the eye. The ears would be pinned back and the lobes diminished, both in thickness and length.

She would fly to Mr. Roche to have her nose straightened and trimmed, since he was the "best nose surgeon in the world." (Her nose, Ruth surmised, was his commission.)

As for her body, loose skin from beneath the arms would be tucked, and fat removed from shoulders, back, buttocks, hips, and belly. If she insisted on leg shortening, the shoulders would be braced back to keep the arms in better proportion to the rest. Ruth frowned when she read this.

She must allow at least two years for these processes to be completed, and four if she wanted her height diminished. The proposed changes were radical and both body and mind would require time to heal. There would be some discomfort. (Ruth knew well enough that what patients feel before an operation is called by surgeons pain: and what they feel after it, discomfort.)

She could come and go at the clinic as she wanted, but there would be many required periods of bed rest, before and after operations. A more detailed program would be drawn up shortly after her arrival, after further physical examinations.

The clinic enclosed a breakdown of approximate fees. The sums required would be roughly $110,000 for the face, $300,000 for the body, and $1,000,000 for the legs. Specialists, as she must realize, would have to be flown in from many countries. There might be grants available from research foundations to help with the latter sum, however.

The making of medical history [Mr. Ghengis wrote in ink at the bottom of the third page of the letter] is not cheap. We'll do the legs last, to give medicine a modest chance to catch up with human aspiration. But you'll be pleased to know there's a new technique developed for removing lengths of vein, heat-sealing the edges. It's been tried with excellent results on cats, but not yet on humans.

Ruth rang the Vesta Rose Agency and was put through to Nurse Hopkins. The agency had its own exchange now, and the young women who manned it—womanned it, as they insisted—were efficient, businesslike, and polite.

"My dear, how are you?"

"My dear, I've missed you so, but I've been too busy to notice."

"Spoken like a man," observed Ruth. "How's the little boy?" She referred to Olga's autistic son.

"Not so little anymore, and very strong," Nurse Hopkins lamented happily.

"But then, so are you!" admired Ruth.

"I know, and I think I have the problem cracked at last. They're trying out a new tranquilizer at Lucas Hill; I can get supplies through one of our staff. It's going to make all the difference to the child. I'm sure of it."

"Do we have anyone in Greenways?" That was the name of Bobbo's prison.

"One of the art therapists, and the governor's secretary. Why?"

"I'd dearly love to meet one of them."

"I'd try the art therapist," said Nurse Hopkins easily. "She has a child in the day-care center. She brings him in extra early. She's a good painter and is trying to get an exhibition together. Her name's Sarah."

Ruth had coffee with Sarah in an out-of-the-way coffeehouse.

She inquired about Bobbo.

"He's settling down," said Sarah, "at last."

"At last?"

"He was quite violent for a while, after his sentence. He's paranoic, of course. He kept saying someone had bribed the judge. I really think he ought to be in Lucas Hill. The border-line between madness and criminality is always so fine."

"At least you get out of Greenways," said Ruth.

"Eventually," Sarah admitted. She was dark and full faced and beautiful. She drank black coffee so as not to put on weight and refused Danish pastries. Sarah observed that Bobbo was now a little depressed. She knew, because of the colors he chose to make his raffia baskets in the art room. She tried to make him use bold, primary colors, but he would stick to the duns and khakis. And his visitors upset him.

"Does he have many visitors?"

"There's a little blond woman comes sometimes."

"No children?"

"No. Probably just as well. It's bad enough when the woman comes. He just stares into space for days afterward."

"Then perhaps she shouldn't come! Why doesn't he write and ask her not to? It's like children in the hospital. They settle so much quicker if their parents don't visit."

Sarah said she thought that was a good idea. She'd suggest it to Bobbo. They were really quite close. They'd work something out together at the moral rejuvenation session on Thursday.

"It sounds like quite a nice prison," said Ruth.

"It is, very," said Sarah. "I don't know why the suicide rate is so high!"

Ruth wrote to the Hermione Clinic, accepting their terms but asking them to set grant aid in motion. It never did to let anyone know that money was not a cause of concern.

She said good-bye to her body. She took off her clothes in the hallway and studied herself in the mirror that stood leaning against a wall, large, gilt-framed, and Georgian. The glass was dark and speckled and chipped, and a crack ran narrowly from one side to another, but the central portion was sufficiently unmarked to throw back a fair reflection.

She looked at the body that had so little to do with her nature, and knew she'd be glad to be rid of it.

Ruth bought a first class ticket to Los Angeles and the Hermione Clinic, and took the next flight out. She had no luggage, other than a few books, bought at the airport. There was nothing from her past that she wanted to bring. Such few telephone numbers as she would need were in her head.

**30** Mary Fisher lives in the High Tower and wishes she didn't. She doesn't want to live anywhere, in fact. Quite frankly, she wants to be dead. She wants to be at one with the stars and the foaming sea, she wishes the flame of her life to burn out and be over, forever. She is romantic, even when suicidal.

Father Ferguson says, "This can't go on, it is a sin."

"I know," says Mary Fisher. She believes in hell now. She is in it already, and knows she deserves it. She has carnal knowledge of a priest!

"You tempted me," he says.

"I know," is all she says. He packs his canvas bag and goes visiting Alice Appleby, whose novels are a success, and whose wise and lovely face stares out from bookracks everywhere. He is not a good lover. He has had so little practice in his life. Perhaps Alice Appleby will do the trick.

Mary Fisher receives a letter from Bobbo asking her not to visit him anymore. "Your visits prevent me from settling. . . ." Mary Fisher thinks somehow he's found out about Harness. She can't get the thought out of her head. She is to blame for this, too. She stops visiting.

She stands at the window of the High Tower and almost jumps. But how can she? She is trapped by her own awareness, her own new understanding, and indeed, her new kindness. How would her mother live without her at the end of her life, or Andy, or Nicola, just emerging into theirs? Mary Fisher must be there to love them, because there is no one else to do it, and perhaps, who knows, no one else ever will. And what sort of example would it be, if she were to hand back the gift of life? It is a baton in a relay race: it must be handed on properly or the whole race stops. Love will be the end of her indeed, but in its own way, its own time.

Mary Fisher isn't feeling well. She looks in the mirror and sees that her hair is thin and her complexion dull. She has lost weight. When she goes down to the village she is just another scurrying, aging woman, holding on to what is left of her life. Eyes slip past her.

The bank writes to tell her she is badly overdrawn. She must put the High Tower on the market. She is not sorry to do so. She tells Garcia and Joan—the only staff left—that they can have no more wages.

"You can't do that," says Garcia.

"I can," she says, staring Garcia straight in the eyes. He drops his. She wonders why she did not do it long ago. What was there ever to be frightened of, except coming face-to-face with her own guilt?

"But where will we live?" ask the children and old Mrs. Fisher. For once they are subdued and kind and likable. "How will we live?"

"As other people do," she said. "In a small and sensible house somewhere. There'll be enough money left over for that."

But it comes too late. She is tired, tired. With success comes failure. Her body has noted her earlier despair, seized its opportunity, returned to disorder, to misrule. The steady flowering pattern has lost its head, spun into disorder. Now cells proliferate without intent, set free like children out of school.

Mary Fisher has a nasty recurring pain across her back. She goes to the doctor. He sends her to hospital for investigation. He does not think the prognosis is good.

She goes into hospital, protesting, saying, just like anyone else, "But I can't possibly go. There's far too much to be done. How will they all get on without me?"

Mary Fisher, without knowing it, is almost happy. If happiness is anything, it is a feeling of being essential.

Would-be purchasers come and look over the High Tower. Property prices have fallen and the cost of gasoline is high. No one really wants to live so far from anywhere: and the cliff face is crumbling, and perhaps soon the whole edifice will topple into the sea. The cost of ensuring it does not will be exorbitant: it is as if nature itself will have to be braced, supported and strengthened, if life is to be tolerable.

**31** Mr. Ghengis enjoyed his work. It seemed to him that it was one of the few occupations in the world that could not be faulted. Social work could be seen as system-bolstering; ordinary doctoring as fostering the interest of the pharmaceutical companies; teaching as the enslavement of the young mind; the arts as idle elitism; business of any kind as grinding the world's poor beneath the capitalist heel; and so forth: but cosmetic surgery was pure. It made the ugly beautiful. To transform the human body, the shell of the soul, was, Mr. Ghengis felt, the nearest a man could get to motherhood: molding, shaping, bringing forth in pain and anguish. True, the pain and anguish were not strictly his but his patients'. Nevertheless, he felt it. Nothing was for nothing.

He thought he would enjoy working with Marlene Hunter. He saw her as a giant parcel to be unwrapped: the kind of parcel that was passed around at a children's birthday party, clumsily wrapped by a kind mother, in layer after layer of crumpled paper, the simpler for inexpert little fingers to unfold. And there, eventually, when the music stopped for the last time, would the treasure be! The gift, the present. He looked forward to it, and to her gratitude.

He showed Miss Hunter to her room himself. It was a gentle lilac color, delicately scented, much like the clinic's writing paper. Drips and respirators and the shiny white apparatus of modern medicine were kept beneath smooth wraps, in a discreet corner. Wide windows looked out over a red desert: in the distance rose a cliff face; an escarpment. In the foreground clustered the rich and luxuriant flora that plentiful water provides in a climate where it does not come naturally, or easily.

"Do you like it?" he asked.

"My mother would have loved it," she replied.

He thought he might leave her vocal chords untautened: a voice that sounded harsh out of a massive frame might sound husky, and by inference sexy, from a slighter one. It was the balance of male and female in the body that attracted, he had observed. A male desire in a fragile body, a deep voice in conjunction with a delicate gesture, and so forth: duplicity and artifice, and not simplicity at all.

Miss Hunter did not choose to mix with her fellow guests. She kept mostly to her room, watching television or flicking through magazines.

"You could learn a language," he suggested, worrying for her. "Why should I?"

"You may want to travel," he said, surprised. "Afterward. People often do. They like to show their new selves off."

"Let them learn to speak my language," she said.

"Well, it would be something to do," he repeated. She made him feel forlorn, as if he were the servant of her desires and not their master. "There's a lot of waiting about in this business. Besides, surely improvement of the mind is a good thing, for its own sake?"

"I am here to improve my body," she replied. "There was never anything wrong with my mind."

He was her Pygmalion, but she would not depend upon him, or admire him, or be grateful. He was accustomed to being loved by the women of his own construction. A soft sigh of adoration would follow him down the corridors as he paced them, visiting here, blessing there, promising a future, regretting a past: cushioning his footfall, and his image of himself. But no soft breathings came from Miss Hunter. Well, he would bring her to it.

He attended to her face first. He padded out the tissue beneath the eyes, just a little, and lifted the fold above them; now less of the white beneath the iris showed, and more above it, so that her eyes suddenly became wide, candid, and innocent, and large in proportion to her head: they were enchanting, as kittens' eyes are enchanting, or indeed the eyes of the young of any species— even of the crocodile.

Mr. Ghengis's assistant, young Dr. Joseph Black, so bold and randy on the baseball field, so delicate and persnickety at the operating table, marveled at the face Miss Hunter aspired to have. They had a blowup of Mary Fisher's photograph, one of those provided by Ruth, projected on the wall in the operating room where they worked.

"It seems a familiar face," said Dr. Black. He recollected where he had seen it—where else but on the back of various book jackets in the clinic library. Not that any of the patients were great readers: they leafed through magazines and complained if they were out-of-date. Only occasionally would one or two of them settle down to a romance or a thriller. But they liked to have the books there; they felt insulted if they were not. They believed themselves to be readers at heart, temporarily resting while under stress.

When Miss Hunter's eyes had healed they broke her cheekbones and flattened them out: and when the bruising had abated somewhat they trimmed and altered the line of the jawbone. They took hairless skin from her rump and grafted it along the hairline, taking it back to give her a smooth, clear brow. They lifted the skin beneath the jaw, stretched it over the cheeks, and tucked it in. They filled fine wrinkle marks around the mouth and nose with silicone and treated broken veins with laser darts. They nicked off the moles, hairs and all, and took the opportunity to tilt the corners of her mouth upward, so that now her expression was one of agreeable expectation.

New teeth were implanted, one by one, in the jaw prepared by Mr. Firth, using a method so tedious and painful it was seldom used. The dental mechanic working from the photograph of Mary Fisher found the teeth were not totally regular; but the imperfections charmed. Bold, strong, even teeth can frighten: they are clearly made for biting rather than lisping.

Now the nose loomed large, hooked and horrific in Miss Hunter's sweet face. The head seemed small in proportion to the body. It was to be expected.

Miss Hunter paid bills monthly, promptly, writing the figure without wincing, although sometimes any physical movement, however small, would cause her exquisite pain. It was as if she insisted that money should be the basis of the transaction between them and not the caring, sharing pleasure of a joint endeavor. It hurt him.

She agreed to fly back to her own country to have her nose seen to. Mr. Roche offered to fly to her, but she said no, she had business to attend to at home. She went on a stretcher, accompanied by medical orderlies.

They reported back to Mr. Ghengis later that, although in great pain, she had appointed agents and seen to the purchase of a property: a dilapidated lighthouse on the edge of a cliff a long way from everywhere.

"I do hope," remarked Dr. Black, "that after all this she isn't going to hide her light under a bushel."

"She'll do what she wants," said Mr. Ghengis. "She'll get what she wants. She is remarkable."

They were both half in love with her. They admitted it to one another. They longed for her return. They did not trust Mr. Roche to do the work properly, worrying that he would be revenged upon her, the way men in positions of medical power are so often revenged upon the women who depend upon them: or so women claim. They had heard it often enough. Naturally enough, they exempted themselves as doctors from this. Dr. Black had a gamine little wife who raised money for the preservation of endangered species all over the world: she was energetic and forthright. He could exercise no power over her, he told Mr. Ghengis, even had he wanted, since she felt more for animals than for humans. A reproachful look from her corgi upset her more than one from her husband. Husbands were two a penny where she came from; they were instantly replaceable and in infinite supply. Mr. Ghengis, of course, was not married. The reason he gave to Dr. Black was that he knew he would, sooner or later, succumb to the urge to make his wife more physically perfect, and that once he had achieved perfection with her he would lose interest. It was the journey, so far as women were concerned, that satisfied. The arrival was anti-climax.

They had a model of Miss Hunter before them as they talked, made in a new transparent substance called Flexiwax, threaded through with plastic sinews and veins and bones: they played with it, pinching out flesh here, adding it there, working their way to perfection. They thought they might have to alter the position of the kidneys, so that they lay one above the other, not side by side. It was easy enough. The working parts of the body must be properly linked; their actual position was immaterial.

Marlene Hunter returned to the desert, on a stretcher, but with a small tip-tilted nose and delicately curved nostrils. The face was a mass of bruising and the eyes lay in black hollows, but she could already be seen to be strikingly pretty.

"Isn't it rather *ordinary*?" worried Dr. Black.

"If you have been extraordinary all your life," reflected Mr. Ghengis, "just to be ordinary must be wonderful."

"But we don't want to make her like the others who come in here."

"Why not?" asked Mr. Ghengis, who prided himself on his perception. "Since that is what she wants; all she has ever wanted is to be like other women."

That June they started on her torso. They fined down and abbreviated the shoulder blades. They made the breasts smaller. They removed flesh from the upper arms and drew the loose skin up into the armpits. They liquidized and drew off fat from the dowager's hump that had developed at the base of her neck. They moved downward. They tautened and lifted her belly and tightened her buttocks. In the end they left her kidneys where they were, too near the surface of her body for safety, but the gestalt of her system was under threat: her heartbeat would slow, then race, even in the interoperative periods. Her menstrual cycle required hormonal topping-up to keep it functioning. It seemed to Mr. Ghengis and Dr. Black the less internal surgery her body was obliged to endure the better. The possible danger to her future health by virtue of a blow to less than adequately protected kidneys was outweighed by this factor. If, at the end of it all, she still had an appetite for surgery, she could have her kidneys moved in her spare time.

Mr. Ghengis tightened Miss Hunter's vagina and drew back the clitoris to heighten his patient's sexual response. This made Dr. Black uneasy.

"It seems an interference with the essential self," he complained.

"There is no such thing as the essential self," said Mr. Ghengis. "It is all inessential, and all liable to change and flux, and usually the better for it."

Miss Hunter needed increasing doses of heroin to dull the pain. Her body had become addicted to the substance, but her mind remained elated and producing the hormones most conducive to her general health. They would cure the addiction when they had to, not before. In the meantime, her will to recover was phenomenal.

Only once did it flag; she received a letter from home, an unusual event. She wept. She lay in bed and her eyes were dull and her hands limp—or such of these as could be seen through the bandages: Mr. Ghengis, recently, had made a series of hairline incisions between the fingers and drawn up the skin over the backs of the hands.

"What's the matter?" he asked.

"Someone I know has cancer," she replied. "She's dying, in the hospital."

"Someone you know well?"

"I met her at a party: we drove home in a car together. And once I went to dinner at her place. That's all."

"She must have made a great impression, to upset you so now."

"Oh, she did."

He said that if Miss Hunter wished, she could return home to see her friend before she died. It would be as well to give her body as long a rest as possible before they started on her legs. If, indeed, wisdom and prudence had not prevailed and Miss Hunter had not changed her mind, and would put up with her legs as they were, and be content to be a statuesque beauty?

But Miss Hunter said she could not waste her time or her life in hospital visiting, and that the leg processes should begin at once, since there was less time than she had thought; and not only were her legs to be tucked, but her arms, too. She did not want to look like a gorilla.

In fact, shortening the arm was simplicity itself compared to shortening the leg. The arms did not have to bear the body's weight. It had just never been done.

"Tell her about the cost!" suggested Dr. Black. "Tell her it is simply not worth it."

But Miss Hunter did not care about money. She used it as a tool to achieve her ends: she despised it. She had invested it well, if speculatively. She had a broker in New York regularly at the end of the telephone: she made killings on the money market. One of the girls on the clinic switchboard, listening in, had invested her small savings, her few miserable hundreds of dollars, as Miss Hunter did; now she had a substantial portfolio and hundreds of thousands to her name.

Miss Hunter believed, as many do who have achieved wealth but who have been born to poverty, that the more you spend the more you get. Mr. Ghengis and Dr. Black gathered their medical team together from the far corners of the earth, and Miss Hunter paid, without flinching. And the more she paid, the happier she seemed.

She was increasingly popular with the nurses and the clinic staff. They admired her courage, and they admired her looks. She was charming. She could not help it. Her face, as it emerged out of bruising and swelling, was set in an expression of sweetness. Her eyes sparkled; her long lashes (grafted from elsewhere) veiled any sharpness of expression; her voice was husky and expressive. They flew, men and women alike, but especially men, to do her bidding.

Dr. Black, deviously, invited Miss Hunter to a party at his home on the eve of the arm operations. It was a fund-raising occasion given by his wife. Dr. Black and Mr. Ghengis hoped that the response to her at the party would be such that she would be content with her new self and leave well alone.

"But I'm not a party kind of person," she objected at first. "I never know what to say."

"Good heavens," said Dr. Black, "someone like you doesn't have to *say* anything. All you have to do is to *be*."

Still she demurred. Mrs. Black telephoned.

"You simply must come," she said. "A party's just the thing for morale. And it's in a good cause. Polar bears. People think that because animals are large they don't need protection, but the opposite is true. Well, you of all people must know that! My husband's told me so much about you."

There was a small silence. Presently Miss Hunter replied, "I should simply love to come, Mrs. Black."

A hairdresser worked for some hours upon Miss Hunter's hair. Now it waved and hung in fashionable gold profusion, looped and tendriled to hide unsightly scars. In fact, the scars all over her body amounted to little more than a tracery of fine white lines. She had healed wonderfully well, doctors and nurses agreed, as if the parted flesh were all too eager to leap together again in its new configuration. In most cosmetic patients wounds seemed determined to mend in the old pattern, not the new, building up scar tissue in an attempt to make things as they had been, not as they now were. The red rims around her eyes had faded and were now scarcely noticeable. She moved a little cautiously still; she spoke tentatively; there was something wonderfully newborn about her.

"She's like Venus," said Dr. Black to his wife, "risen freshly from her conch shell. Enchanting!"

Mrs. Black marveled at how impressionable men were, even doctors. Like show-biz producers, they would stop to gape at the stars that they themselves had made.

Miss Hunter was late arriving at the party. The young Californian chauffeur delegated to collect her in the clinic's pale mauve limousine was taking her by the long scenic route to show her the beauties of nature. Mr. Ghengis, made vaguely jealous, and not convinced that his patient's intimate parts were yet fully healed, drank too much champagne and embarrassed the other guests, who were mostly of the medical establishment. It was an area of the country much given over to private medical clinics. Land was cheap and the views superb.

"I am her Pygmalion," he cried. "I made her, and she is cold, cold! Where is Aphrodite, to breathe her into life?" He searched the party for someone yet more beautiful than his creation, and could not find anyone.

"Only man is vile," said Mrs. Black, with passion. "If we leave that beast alone it will leave us alone."

It was apparent to Mrs. Black that Miss Hunter was to be the star attraction at her party, whether she liked it or not. From her husband's account of what was going on at the clinic, she quite expected to see a female version of Frankenstein's monster appear, with the plates of her scalp pinned together with iron bolts. Mrs. Black frequently called her husband Frankenstein over the breakfast table, or last thing at night, when he was preparing himself for sleep. "Good night, Frankenstein." They had married each other in an idealistic flurry: she to save the wildlife of the world, he to eradicate human disease. Now they lived in a house with lilac drapes and picture windows with a desert view, and he spent his life defying nature, not flowing with it, and their children ate pink food, like anyone else's, and the human and the animal race went to hell.

Miss Hunter entered. Heads turned. Mrs. Black stepped forward to greet her. Her guest was dressed in gold lamé, in a manner that Mrs. Black—who wore designer jeans and white voile shirts to parties—personally found distasteful; the dress hugged her figure to the hips, and flared thereafter, falling a surprisingly long way down to rather large feet. A little fur bolero and a gold strap or two about the shoulders and arms served to cover scars, but only those in the know would have realized that, presumed Mrs. Black. Miss Hunter reminded Mrs. Black of an illustration in one of the old *Esquires* of her youth brought back to life: an impossible male fantasy made flesh.

Miss Hunter said she was chilly; she would keep her fur. Her voice was agreeably husky. The division between her breasts was wide, and at eye level, for those on the shorter side. Men stared, and clustered, and stared again, and the bolder sought to draw her aside and make assignations, which she declined, saying sweetly that she was temporarily out of circulation, and they mustn't mind, or be jealous. But they did, and they were.

Mrs. Black said to Dr. Black, "She is an insult to womanhood. What's more, she looks much like anyone else, only taller, and to all accounts even that won't be for long. You and your friends aren't doctors. You are reductionists."

"It's what she wanted," said Dr. Black.

"I suppose what she thought was," observed Mrs. Black, "if you can't beat them, join them."

"I'd rather not talk about it," said Dr. Black, stiffly. "What you are witnessing is the making of medical history, but of course that cuts no ice with you."

Mr. Ghengis circled Miss Hunter as a sculptor might circle his finished creation. Everything worked. Her eyes shone and glittered; her lips were moist. She raised a glass of champagne, she sipped. He knew her jaw still ached with movement but that she was too proud, too stubborn, to show the pain. Just sometimes it was her habit to let out a little sound, half-groan, half-sigh, the same ingoing and outgoing of breath as a grieving woman might utter in lovemaking, of pain and relief combined, that seemed to be both summoned out of a dreadful past and called back from an unholy future.

The wide windows were open; the drapes stirred in the hot night air. He loved her. She would never be grateful. He did not expect gratitude anymore. He had made her as a mother makes a child: to be its own self, not hers. And, as is usual in a successfully reared child, she was indifferent to her parent.

"You'll have to marry me," he said to her. "We'll have to have children."

"But I don't want children," she said. "I am busy earning the present, not the future."

Dr. Black, overhearing the proposal, and feeling that his colleague was taking an unfair advantage, if only in presuming on his unmarried state, took offense and tried to hit Mr. Ghengis, succeeding only in knocking off Mr. Ghengis's glasses and falling among the vegetarian curry and nutty chick-pea salad. A fellow guest, darting backward as bottles fell and glasses broke, trampled on Mr. Ghengis's glasses and shattered them.

Mrs. Black, who had hoped to do her fund-raising a little later in the evening, understood that her efforts would now be wasted and that the party, which she had never wanted to give in the first place, was a disaster. Guests were already leaving with that particular party-leaving politeness that means there will be giggles and gossip the next day. Only Miss Hunter, of course, lingered.

"You must be satisfied now," Dr. Black was saying to this blond, simpering doll on stilts, "if grown men are fighting over you. Leave your legs as they are. You are beautiful, you are popular, you can go to a party and cause infinite trouble: you are the showgirl type. The balding businessman's dream. We'll reduce the thighs and slim the calves, of course, but have mercy on us. Don't make us attack the bone. It isn't too late. We can pay the team off. You must understand, it's risky. You might even die."

Miss Hunter looked at Dr. Black and shook her head. "You are a very, very naughty boy," she said, and her voice sounded as Mary Fisher's had, long ago. "Breaking Mr. Ghengis's glasses like that!"

"He has another pair," said Dr. Black, almost weeping, and Miss Hunter, under Mrs. Black's nose, beckoned him out onto the balcony, and there they sat, cuddling, as if Mrs. Black didn't exist at all, under the velvet canopy of night, where the stars hung like lanterns. So, once, Mary Fisher would have behaved.

Mrs. Black, washing up glasses, resolved never to give another party, never, and to divorce her husband and next time marry someone without hypocrisy, possibly from the army, who understood how much more satisfactory it is to kill and die for a cause, in the shadow of some great loyalty, than to try to live forever in the framework of the personal and the trivial. Presently Dr. Black drove Miss Hunter back to the clinic, but not before accusing Mrs. Black of unforgivable rudeness to his guest.

**32** The High Tower is empty, and silent, except for the wind, which rustles up and down the stairs, in through the empty space where once the great front door stood, and Ruth knocked and the Dobermans barked and the traitor Garcia opened and the end began. Then out goes the wind through a broken windowpane or two. Passing dealers have removed the door, and wandering boys aim stones at the windows. No one likes an empty building. Why should they? It is a rebuke to aspiration. Decay invites dereliction, and vice versa. No one quite believes the "Sold" sticker pasted over the board that says "For Sale." The tower perches too near the edge of the cliff, and the cliff crumbles. Either the cliff has stepped backward, out of the sea, or the tower forward, toward it. Enough to make anyone nervous.

Mice run in and out of the rooms, and fleas, after the cat and dogs went, made the old carpets flicker and jump for a while. But now they've given up and gone. Slugs move happily about the stone kitchen floor.

Perhaps it was better before. Perhaps anything is better than peace.

Mary Fisher lingers on in the hospital. Her hair has fallen out, as a result of treatment. Garcia and Joan have gone, taking their baby with them, the hole in its heart mended with the last of Mary Fisher's money. They have gone to live with Garcia's mother in Spain, to comfort her in her old age, with the money saved and stolen by her son over the dancing years. Nicola lives in the village with the science teacher from her school: one Lucy Barker. Nicola loves only women. Andy works as a garage mechanic. His boss has taken him in to live, out of kindness. Andy is indistinguishable from the village boys; he hangs around street corners and longs vaguely for a life he will never have.

I visited the High Tower when I was having my nose done. I drove through the village in my Rolls-Royce, and by chance I saw Andy, emerging oil-stained from beneath a parked car. I knew he was my son, but I felt nothing. He is nothing to do with me. And I waited outside the house where Nicola lives and saw her emerge: she has Bobbo's frown and my build. She lurches and lurks; there was a sullen content about her. She will never make a she-devil. My children have been sucked back into the sea of ordinary humanity, swirled down and under, and are back where they belong: they are unspectacular and, I imagine, quite content.

Old Mrs. Fisher, obliged to look after herself, does very well, better than her daughter, which was always her ambition. She lives in the district where she was born, on her own, and manages very well. She visits her daughter once a week. A smelly, waddling visitor, she is feared by the nurses and shakes her head over her daughter and suggests that her illness is the wages of sin. Mary Fisher smiles and pats the old hand that once nursed her. The sister of the ward is a mature woman, whose first steps back into the world, when wifehood and motherhood were at an end, were through the Vesta Rose Agency. She is fond of Mary Fisher. She looks after her well.

Mary Fisher is not visited by Bobbo, although surely, on compassionate grounds (for she is dying) they would let him out to do so if he asked. He wants nothing more to do with her. He loved her, and love failed. But he blames Mary Fisher, not love, as he should.

I stand at the foot of the High Tower and I look out to sea, which is impervious to human influence, and I look inland over the fields and hills, which are not, and which take the beauty into themselves that human eyes grant them. Mary Fisher, in losing this landscape, had added to its loveliness. I know that; I always have. How could Mr. Ghengis and Dr. Black have given me beauty, except through love?

I will build up the High Tower. I will tear up the clumps of grass that now grow between the paving stones. I will shore up the cliff, making it safe, but I will look mostly inland and not to sea. I will look out, as Mary Fisher looked out from her bedroom window, sitting up after a night of love with her Bobbo—my Bobbo—to where the new morning sun glances over hills and valleys and trees, and know, as she did, that it is beautiful, and make this my acknowledgment of her, my grief for her, all that I have to give her. She is a woman: she made the landscape better. She-devils can make nothing better, except themselves. In the end, she wins.

**33** On the night of the party Ruth returned to her chaste room at the clinic and refused Dr. Black admittance. Mrs. Black, said Ruth, with some complacency, would be upset if her husband did not return with reasonable promptness.

Ruth closed her eyes for sleep with the comfortable thought that for a pretty woman the future lay in refusing men rather than submitting to them—or, indeed, hoping for their advances. As a corollary, she reflected, perhaps only a plain woman would be in a position to develop sexual expertise and an appetite for sexual pleasure, as a pretty one would not; but Ruth had had, after all, years enough in which to practice and acquire the latter. She would have the best of all worlds, of heaven and hell. She slept well.

It was the last time Ruth was to sleep soundly for many, many months. The discomfort described by her doctors amounted to acute pain; increasing doses of morphia and major tranquilizers clouded her mind but could not sever the connection between sensation and response. She did not, in fact, wish to be free from the pain: pain, she knew, was the healing agent. It marked the transition from her old life to her new one. She must endure it now, to be free of it hereafter. In most lives pain drags itself out, a twinge here, a discomfort there, idly distributing itself throughout a lifespan. Ruth would have it all now and be done with it. Yet she was aware that it might kill her in transit, so concentrated was it in its sweep and power.

She screamed in the night, sometimes. They kept pills safely locked up and the windows were laced with elegant steel bars. Not that her plastered legs would take her anywhere, but one never knew. She was not, they had come to the conclusion, an ordinary person. If she could not use her legs, perhaps she might choose to walk on her hands?

There was an earthquake, a nasty rumble, the crust of the earth yearning to split along the line of its weakness, the San Andreas fault. That was the day after the major operation on her femur was performed: life-support systems had to be switched over to the emergency generator. They thought they would lose her in the seconds it took. Ruth observed their pallor, their distraction. When she could speak she said, "You needn't have worried. An act of God won't kill me."

"Why not?" aked Mr. Ghengis. "I don't imagine He's on your side."

"He has the Devil to contend with," said Ruth, before lapsing back into unconsciousness.

Mr. Ghengis begged her to be content with two and a half inches taken from the femur but she would not.

A violent electrical storm on the eve of the second major operation shorted the power supply again. Such storms were not unusual in the area. The sudden darkening of the day, the violent clouds tumbling through the unnatural dark, the rifts of sudden, piercing light: but this was, unusually, a dry storm. No rain fell to gladden the heart hereafter, in the sudden sprouts of green and general giddiness that could be expected to compensate for the earlier terror.

"God's angry," said Mr. Ghengis, suddenly frightened, longing to go back into obstetrics. "You're defying Him. I wish we could stop all this."

"Of course He's angry," said Ruth. "I am remaking myself."

"We're remaking you," he said sourly, "and in one of His feebler and more absurd images, what's more." He had come to hate the photograph of Mary Fisher.

Electricians worked all through the night checking the circuits that worked the pumps and levers and valves that could imitate, if only temporarily, and on a part-by-part basis, not as a gestalt, the workings of the human body.

"The only thing we can't control," said Mr. Ghengis, "is the spark, the little spark of life. But we're working on it. And of course the weather."

"You're going to have trouble with your legs for the rest of your life," Mr. Ghengis warned her, for the last time. "You'll have to be on blood-thinning medication; there'll always be a danger of clotting; and God knows how the abbreviated arteries will hold —the muscles will probably go into spasm. You're mad."

That morning she had a financial report from her advisers. "Then I am a mad multimillionairess," she said, "and you will do as I say."

Medical journalists, of the kind who roam the surgeries of the world in search of yet more bizarre transplants and the laboratories in search of two-headed dogs and giant mice, congregated around the clinic. But Ruth had covered her tracks well; they could find out nothing about her, neither her nationality, her marital status, nor her age. She was a woman who wanted to be shorter: that was all they knew. They stole the clinic's records, but could find no history for Marlene Hunter. There was a flurry of articles and features on height as a function of character and a molder of personality; on short men who became generals and tall women who became nobody, and on which came first, looks or personality. How dogs grew to look like their masters; wives and husbands like each other; adopted children like adoptive parents. These facts were discussed and dismissed, since there was nothing anyone could do about them. The world lost interest.

Ruth hovered, moaning, drifting, on the edge of life and death. Another electrical storm seemed to stimulate her into life; lightning hit the clinic's TV aerial and for at least six hours there was no TV reception. Ruth opened her eyes at the initial bang and during the next few hours her temperature fell to normal, her blood pressure rose, her heart steadied, and she sat up and demanded food. Dr. Black, who had dropped the image of Venus on her conch since Ruth's rejection of him, was heard to refer to her as Frankenstein's monster, something that needed lightning to animate it and get it moving. He was assumed to be referring to Mr. Ghengis as Frankenstein, not himself; the relationship between the two men had deteriorated recently.

It was nine months before Ruth could take so much as a step. Mr. Ghengis wanted to wait for a further three months before beginning on the arms, but she insisted that they be done at once. She was, she said, beginning to be bored.

She had relented and learned French, Latin, and Indonesian during her convalescence. She had given herself courses in world literature and art appreciation. She had done all the sensible things his patients always believed they would do when confined to bed and with time to spare, but almost never did. There had been one attempted suicide on her account, by a young trainee nurse whose doctor boyfriend used to linger overlong in Ruth's room.

Ruth received a letter from home, black-edged. It was from Garcia. This time she did not weep, she smiled. "My friend is dead," she said. "Long live my friend."

She flew home for the funeral; she made much use of a wheelchair, but every day could take a step or two more and use her hands more freely. She had lost sensation in two fingers and the scarring on legs and upper arms was still noticeable. It was winter; it did not matter. She was rich enough, in any case, to follow winter around the world, if it suited her. She measured, in height, five feet six and a half inches, and around the bust, thirty-eight inches, the waist twenty-four inches, and the hips thirty-seven. Cortisone injections, given at intervals, gave her pretty face a childish innocence, subverting the harshness of experience, and kept her hair luxuriant.

Ruth went to Mary Fisher's funeral wearing silky black, and diamonds. She went in a Rolls-Royce, and did not get out, but watched the funeral from a distance, sitting in the car. The cemetery was by the sea: wind blew spray against the windows. The words of the preacher were forced back into his mouth. A handful of people, a few old friends and former colleagues, gazed and tried to listen. Old Mrs. Fisher, ever curious, came over to Ruth's car to investigate, and stared in through the glass with rheumy eyes, and gestured to Ruth to wind down the window. Ruth obliged, though she did it by pressing a button.

"I thought it was her for a moment," said old Mrs. Fisher. "Just like her to send her own ghost to her funeral! Poor little slut. Well, out of the slime, back to it. But I saw her out! I always knew I would." And she hunched back into the wind, to her daughter's graveside, where Ruth thought she saw her weeping.

Nicola and Andy were not present. They were not, after all, flesh and blood. And had Mary Fisher not destroyed their home, their mother and their father? Make amends even as Mary Fisher had, these things could not be undone.

Bobbo was there, between two warders. He was not handcuffed; there was obviously no need. His eyelids had thickened, and his hair turned gray. He seemed to be sleepwalking, unable to comprehend the meaning of the open grave, or indeed of anything much. He saw Ruth on the arm of her chauffeur.

"Who are you?" he asked.

"I'm your wife," she said, and held him with her young, enchanting eyes, and smiled her sweet new smile.

"My wife died," he said, "long ago."

He seemed to want to move away, and turned, but the warders took an arm each, alert to his sudden animation, and held him so that he had no choice but to look at her again.

"You are my wife," he said. "I'm sorry. I seem to have trouble remembering things. But there was someone called Mary Fisher. Aren't you her?"

"This is Mary Fisher's funeral," said one of the warders, as if to a child. "So how can that be Mary Fisher?"

They apologized to Ruth and took their prisoner, who was by now clearly upset, away. He needed, they felt, more sedation. He was being treated for depression, as it was, with electric shock therapy.

Bobbo was glad to go. The outside world was always full of dreams—flickering out of vision and into nightmare and back again. Prison at least was real, and safe.

Ruth employed good lawyers, who set about securing Bobbo's release. She considered returning the capital sum originally embezzled, but decided against it. Serene men of good intention now ran the parole board: they were not concerned with money any more than Ruth was with abstract virtue. Bobbo would be set free soon enough.

She employed architects and builders; carpenters, plasterers, bricklayers, and plumbers to work on the High Tower. Constructional engineers, shoring up the cliff, had managed marginally to alter the configuration of the entire harbor so that the force of the waves was no longer directed at the tower. So teatime would be less dramatic, but at least safe. She employed a landscape designer and a handful of jobbing gardeners to restore the beauty of the grounds. She paid them well. The front door was replaced—the architect found a sturdy chapel door that fitted well and looked good. She traced and brought back the Dobermans and had both animals neutered. Advancing age had now sobered them considerably. She wrote to Garcia, asking if he would consider returning to the tower to work.

A letter presently came from Garcia accepting Miss Hunter's offer of employment. He would come without wife and child, however: they would stay behind in Spain to keep his old mother company.

Ruth returned to the Hermione Clinic for continued physiotherapy and a few minor bodily adjustments: an ingrowing toenail was seen to; broken veins on the cheeks needed more laser treatment; facial moles kept struggling to reappear.

"First in," as Mr. Ghengis remarked, "last out."

Dr. Black had handed in his notice. He and Mrs. Black were going to the Third World: he to work among deprived and underprivileged humans, she among the crocodiles.

"If he wants to waste his God-given talents doing what any half-trained nurse could do," Mr. Ghengis remarked, "that's up to him."

It seemed to Ruth that at last the time had come to return to the High Tower. She could walk with ease, even run a little. She could lift a two-pound weight in either hand. Her circulatory problems were under control. She no longer needed the Hermione Clinic. She no longer needed anyone. She danced with Mr. Ghengis in the dew of the morning, as the sun rose red and round over the escarpment, and with every step it was as if she trod on knives; but she thanked him for giving her life and told him she was going.

**34** Now I live in the High Tower, and the sea surges beneath as the moon circles and the earth turns, but not quite as it did. Garcia has to clean a different set of windows; the spray falls differently: he marvels at it. Even nature bows to my convenience. I pay him the same as did his previous employer. What was once too much is now too little: inflation has eaten away at its value, but he doesn't realize it and I haven't told him. Why should I? If you want to keep servants you must treat them badly. The same, I find, applies to lovers.

Garcia comes often to my bedroom at night, knocking and whispering with love. Just occasionally I let him in. I make sure Bobbo knows, and suffers; that is the only pleasure I take in Garcia's body. To join with him is a political, not a sexual act, for me if not for him. How emotional men are!

Bobbo loves me, poor confused creature that he has become, pouring my tea, mixing my drinks, fetching my bag. He has us both in the one flesh: the one he discarded, the one he never needed after all. Two Mary Fishers. His eyes grow dull, as if he were already an old man. That is what humiliation does. He could have something done about his thickening eyelids, of course; he could have plastic surgery and be young again, but he would have to ask me for the money. I wait for him to suggest it, but he doesn't. How weak people are! How they simply accept what happens, as if there were such a thing as destiny, and not just a life to be grappled with.

Sometimes I let Bobbo sleep with me. Or I take my lovers in front of him. What agreeable turmoil that causes in the household! Even the dogs sulk. I cause Bobbo as much misery as he ever caused me, and more. I try not to, but somehow it is not a matter of male or female, after all; it never was: merely of power. I have all, and he has none. As I was, so he is now.

Good. Life is very pleasant. I sit up in bed in the morning and look out over the landscape. Some people say I've ruined it, with artificial copses and granite-fountained fish ponds and the rest, but I like it. Nature gets away with far too much. It needs controlling. I have many friends. I am very hospitable and charming, and there's always a nervy excitement at my parties. The food's superb. There is smoked salmon and champagne for those who care for that kind of thing—I have rather more Eastern and exotic tastes myself.

I tried my hand at writing a novel and sent it to Mary Fisher's publishers. They wanted to buy it and publish it, but I wouldn't let them. Enough to know I can do it, if I want. It was not so difficult after all; nor she so special.

I am a lady of six foot two, who had tucks taken in her legs. A comic turn, turned serious.

ABOUT THE AUTHOR

FAY WELDON was born in England and raised in New Zealand. She has an M.A. in economics and psychology, and before turning to the writing of books, film scripts, and plays, she pursued a highly successful career in advertising. Her previous books include *Puffball, Praxis, Words of Advice, Female Friends,* and *Down Among the Women.* Her novels have been translated into eleven foreign languages, and her stage plays have been performed throughout the world.